dual wielding

Three Player Tag-Team Book 2

allyson lindt

acelette press

contents

For my alpha and beta readers, who hold my hand through every book.

But not for my cats, who insist on being held, regardless of deadlines. I love you, babies, but…

And for my eternal dragon.

1 /
brandon

Who spent the day after Thanksgiving at a casino just barely on the Nevada side of the border it shared with Utah, playing video poker?

Far more people than I imagined.

If they were in the casino auditorium with me, they may be smiling more too. Especially once tonight's show hit the stage.

When Danny and Reese heard they'd been booked in Wendover, they were thrilled. Some big-name bands played in the concert hall here, and their band, Plaid Peanut Butter, would scream for an audience of a thousand.

I thought they should be playing to stadiums with fifty times that many, but what I thought should happen and what their band manager made happen were two very different things. Which was why I was sitting in a room that could maybe hold 200, wasn't anywhere near at capacity, and a lot of the people who were here had stumbled in looking for a place to sit for a minute.

The lights dimmed and my anticipation grew. It didn't matter where Plaid Peanut Butter played, I always loved their shows. I was the ultimate fanboy-slash-roadie. Hell, I was fucking a member of the band.

"Ladies and gentlemen, welcome to Wendover." Reese's voice came over the sound system. "Are you ready to *rock* with Plaid Peanut Butter?"

I whooped and whistled and clapped, and most of the other people in the room joined in, as the opening riffs to *Welcome to the Jungle* filled the room, and Danny walked on stage as he played. So sexy. He was a few inches taller than my 5'11", and on stage that height let him tower over everyone. His short, dirty blond hair was carelessly mussed, and combined with the guitar and faded T-shirt, gave him that perfect bad-boy rocker look.

He wasn't much of a bad-boy, but I loved the look anyway.

The screaming that bled into the chords was Reese. So were the drums, but those were part of a pre-recorded track. She strode into the spotlight to join Danny, and as he slid into the song, she belted out the lyrics in a voice Axel Rose only wished he had. The outfit she wore on stage was made to draw attention. A long lavender wig, purple glasses and boots, and a leather jacket that hugged her body and showed off generous cleavage.

They always opened with a cover, to draw people into the familiar before mixing their own original music. Reese could cover anyone from Halestorm to Evanescence to Guns n Roses in the same set, but the songs she wrote with Danny blew everything else out of the water—Reese with the music and Danny with lyrics that lit the soul on fire.

In fact, I'd met him years ago when he was singing at an open mic night. The words were beauty personified, mostly spoken to a few strummed chords on an acoustic guitar. I'd been smitten from the moment I heard him, and had to introduce myself.

Was I one hundred percent biased when it came to Danny's genius? Yes. But I was also right.

The house lights came on full force, and I winced at the abrupt brightness, amid a series of groans. To their credit, Reese and Danny kept playing, but the sound had been cut too. Still, their voices carried through the room. Even without mics, in a brightly lit room, they emitted sparks.

The side doors to the room slammed open, and three police officers strode in with a man in the casino's branded vest. "We need everyone to stay seated for a moment, please," one of the officers said.

Two more officers stepped in through each of the other doors, blocking the exits.

That couldn't be good.

The small group looked around the room, and I couldn't help but do the same. At least five people were slouched and looking painfully conspicuous in their attempts to vanish into their seats.

The casino employee pointed, and the officers with him nodded. "Gary Rice?" One of them asked. "We need you to come with us."

Every head swiveled as an officer strode toward a young man by himself. "What's up?" Gary's voice shook with the question.

"ID please."

Gary pulled a blue Velcro wallet from his back pocket, looking paler with each passing second. "Did I do something wrong?"

"That's most likely between you and your mother." The officer handed his ID back. "She filed a missing persons report when you didn't come back on the bus with the rest of your Flight Club."

Gary laughed nervously, and left with the officers.

I heard several sighs of relief when the doors closed and no one else was taken out. Danny and Reese really needed to start playing better venues. Not necessarily because of the fans, but this entire gig screamed *lack of care*. Like most of their shows.

"Come on, let's rock," I shouted as much for the benefit of whoever was controlling the lights as for PPB.

The lights stayed on.

Several people stood and wandered toward the exits.

"Hey, guys." Reese's voice wasn't as loud as I expected. The sound hadn't been turned back on yet either.

Danny whistled sharply, and the sound carried through the room.

"We're gonna take a short break, but we'll be back." Reese's yell was much easier to hear.

A few people paused, but most shook their heads and left.

The hard set of Reese's jaw was obvious from here, and I didn't blame her. I made my way to the stage. If this were a proper show, if they were getting the attention they deserved, there would be security to step in my path, but no one stopped me from reaching the band.

Danny let his guitar hang around his neck, and stepped closer to me. I brushed my lips over his. "You sound good tonight."

"We *sounded* good tonight." Reese grabbed her phone from the back pocket of her jeans. "I'm calling Todd."

Todd was their band manager.

"I'll go find someone to turn the lights off and the sound back on." I squeezed Danny's hand, and walked away.

More than a decade ago, before I had any idea

who Plaid Peanut Butter was, Danny and Reese had been playing to packed clubs, and online video was the perfect Wild West for them to get their sound out to the world.

Todd got to them first. He convinced Reese she was the star of the show. That she'd do much better without Danny. She could have a full back-up band, record contracts... Todd sold her on the full package.

Each employee I found, I asked if they could point me toward the person who could get the lights and sound fixed in the lounge. All of them shook their heads.

I was careful to never say so in front of Danny or Reese, but her breaking up the band was the best thing that ever happened to me, and the biggest mistake she ever made. The fallout almost destroyed Danny, and I hated that, but I wouldn't have met him otherwise. I was his salvation and he was my universe.

On the other hand, Reese had gotten herself stuck in a shitty contract she couldn't get out of. One that prohibited any performances or recordings of performances, or basically anything with her singing voice attached to it, from being played unless Todd made the arrangements.

I finally found the guy who had been with the police. I was close enough to see his name tag. "Gordon, hey, how's it going tonight?"

He looked startled to be addressed in such a direct and friendly manner. "Good? Can I help you?"

"Yeah. We need you to turn the lights off and the sound back on in the lounge, so the show can continue."

"I can't do that."

Not what I expected. "Do you need manager approval? Who can I talk to?"

"No and no one. I mean I'm not capable of doing that," he said. "I have to wait until our tech guy calls me back."

"But you turned them off."

He shrugged. "There's an emergency switch. But no one here knows how to start them back up again. We had a new smart system installed a few months ago, and only our tech guy knows how to use it."

I could yell at him, but it wasn't his fault. "How much to let me take a look?" I wasn't the most tech savvy person among our group of friends, but I'd been working with programmers for two decades, and had picked a few things up.

"I can't do that."

My wallet was already in my hand. "You sure? Hundred bucks? Two?"

He shook his head. "Not worth my job. You know this place has cameras everywhere. It'll happen when it happens."

"Not good enough." I hated not having control of a situation, and if this guy wasn't the person to give it to me, he'd tell me who was. "Give me your manager's name."

"There's not one working tonight."

That was either bullshit or stupid. I didn't care which. I grabbed my phone. "Give me the number of the person you call in an emergency, then." I was already swiping in the name of the casino, looking for high level contacts. "Or I'll call Tony Beck directly."

"No one on call," Gordon said.

I clenched my jaw, and pulled the number I'd found up in my phone.

"Is there a problem, sir?" A new voice interrupted and I turned to see a man about as tall as me, but a bit broader in the chest. SECURITY was stamped across the front of his shirt.

Classy. Subtle. Not.

"There is a problem. I was enjoying the concert, and now they can't keep playing. I was about to call the owner, and talk to him about it."

Security scowled. "I need to ask you to leave."

"Why?" I hit *dial* on my phone, and put it to my ear.

"Sir. Please." Security didn't make it sound like a request.

The call went straight to voicemail with a generic greeting, and I snarled. I could leave a ranty message, but that didn't hold the same satisfaction or chance of getting things done. Especially not immediately.

I hung up. "I'm not breaking any rules. I'm looking to resolve an issue."

"Sir."

I stared at him, my irritation shifting closer to anger with each breath. This was ridiculous and infuriating. Rebellion whispered inside—the same itch I'd had for weeks that was extra potent tonight—what would happen if I punched him?

Reality screamed into my brain. I didn't know how to fight, and I suspected he'd hit harder. It was unlikely the police had all left the building.

I clenched my jaw. Threatening to leave a bad review of this shitty place hardly seemed effective, and it definitely wouldn't be satisfying.

Security took a step forward.

"Fine. I'm leaving." I hated the way the resignation tasted. As I walked toward the nearest exit, I texted Danny to let him know I'd be outside. Security followed me the entire way.

Danny's reply came through as I stepped through the door. *We're by the SUV.*

They must not have had any more luck than I did.

Reese's contract only applied to her, but when she and Danny made things right about seven years ago, he started singing with her again. Neither of them performed the same without the other, and he wasn't in it for the fame or money. He just wanted to write and play.

Despite everything, there were times when I envied Reese. She made up her mind as she went along. She chose things because they called to her. Other people's expectations seemed to be the last thing she considered when she made a decision. She probably would've decked Security. Regretted it after, but still…

And I doubted she ever sat down at the piano and asked herself if she was too old to learn to be spontaneous. I doubted she plucked out a few chords and then stopped because it sounded the same as every other piece I'd composed for the video games I wrote music for.

My composer's block had grown to infuriating levels over the past few months, and some days I felt like calling it quits as far as work was concerned. This burnout needed me to break free and do something new.

Unlike Reese, I'd spent most of my life picking up the pieces for a family who chased whims and discarded the rest. I was the responsible one.

Maybe when we were done for the night, I'd do something wild and drop a grand at the tables. It wasn't that I was wealthy, but a stable job, savings, and Christmas bonus meant I could afford things like that sometimes. The carelessness might scratch the impulsive itch.

Except that Reese was hurting for money. She was too proud to accept any help, but dropping that kind of money in front of her, on something so frivolous, would be beyond rude.

And there was my sense of obligation again. Damn it.

I'd find a way to let loose while we were here. Somehow. Somewhere.

I found Danny and Reese waiting next to my Explorer. They didn't have any of their gear on them, so it was either loaded up, or they had to leave it behind. If the casino had Danny's Les Paul, I was definitely picking a fight to get it back.

"We're ready to go." Danny nodded at the back of the truck, meaning their stuff was packed away.

Good. But also a teensy bit disappointing that the performance was over. "No luck with Todd?"

"What do you think?" Reese asked flatly.

Ugh, I needed to blow off some steam, but didn't know where. "Dinner?"

"I need to change first." Reese gestured at her costume.

"That's a given," Danny agreed.

Fortunately, we had reservations somewhere else. Their playing didn't include rooms for the night, and if I was paying, I was staying somewhere I didn't expect roaches as guests. Reese was crashing in our room. She'd given up arguing a while ago that I picked up the tab while they were on the road.

We drove a whole two blocks to where we were staying, and headed to our room.

As we stepped inside, Reese was already stripping off the lavender wig she performed in. She moved into the bathroom to brush out her hair.

"Think if I offered Todd the blowjob of a lifetime, and delivered, he'd put in at least a little effort for our next booking?" The acoustics of tile and Formica distorted her voice and put a warped spin on her sarcasm.

I couldn't sit. Too much unease bounced inside me. "Somehow I don't think a lack of being blown is his problem. I'm not saying he is or isn't getting enough, just that the two probably aren't related."

I pulled Danny close, inhaling the scents of sweat and cologne with anticipation. Maybe we could stay in and fuck. Reese was welcome to watch; she had before.

"Maybe it's worth a shot," Reese said. "I do have magical lips."

I wouldn't argue that her mouth made beautiful sounds, but that wasn't what she was saying. "But are they *get off your ass and do your fucking job* lips?" I asked.

Danny shook his head, a smile on his face, and kissed me playfully before moving out of reach. At least he was enjoying some of this. The banter or the physical touch? I wasn't sure.

Reese emerged from the bathroom, the leather jacket from her stage outfit dangling from one finger. Which left her in a tank top that showed off generous cleavage, and those sexy as fuck jeans. She looked at Danny. "Magical lips. Yes or no?"

He held up his hands in surrender. "Yes. But also, I'm not saying anything."

"Excuse me?" I feigned disbelief. This conversation was ridiculous, but I liked the underlying challenge with Reese. And that disquieted part of me insisted this had the potential to escalate. "I have amazing lips too."

"Also true," Danny said. "But I'm still staying out of this conversation."

Reese smirked and focused on me. "You would not out-blow me."

I'd probably given as many blow jobs as she had, especially considering the kinds of things my colleagues and I got up to at the first software company I worked for, but me insisting she was wrong didn't prove anything. It only prolonged the argument. I itched for action. "Put your money where your mouth is."

"I'm not blowing you." Reese scoffed.

The night was still young. "A kiss. Simple as that. To prove which one of us has more magical lips."

She should shut me down right about now, but

she was more competitive than I was. I'd been stupid to suggest anything, but the proposal was out there and now I was thinking about it the results. What did Reese kiss like?

She twisted her mouth and furrowed her brow. "Intriguing. I kiss you, you kiss me, and... ?"

It wasn't my best thought out plan—unusual for me—but I couldn't let the idea go. This was a bet and we needed stakes. "If you can convince me you're such a great kisser, I'll go Christmas shopping at the mall with the two of you." She started pushing the idea a month ago. To wear me down, I assume.

"Fine." Reese flipped her brown hair over one shoulder, watching me the entire time. "If you prove you're Mister Master Mouth, I'll play your game."

She meant the MMO I'd written the music for. The one that was currently in beta, that she'd been avoiding for months.

"I'm doing some math here, don't hate me," Danny said, "And that means technically you could both win."

"Technically, yes." I wasn't so completely reckless that I'd fuck things up with him, though. "You okay with this?"

He snorted. "Seriously?" Danny was an unabashed voyeur.

"Yes, seriously." For that moment, all of the playfulness vanished from Reese's voice.

"Fucking *hot*," Danny said. "Yes. I'm great with it. Make out until your hearts are content."

This was such a bad idea.

Let's hear it for impulsiveness. I looked at Reese again and gave a deep bow. "Ladies first." I straightened again to find her standing *right there*.

She looked up at me through heavy lashes, her bottom lip caught between her teeth. Her cheeks glistened with the sheen of body glitter, and she almost looked magical. She danced her nails up my stomach with such a light touch, I wasn't sure she made contact, and rested her palm on my chest.

When she tilted her head up, my pulse spiked in anticipation, and when she brushed her lips lightly over mine, all the blood rushed to my cock. She smirked, and bit my bottom lip hard enough to make me grunt in surprise.

Fuck that felt good. She pressed in harder, deepening the kiss. The blend of soft and demanding had me rock hard. How did this feel so incredible?

If we let this go too long, I was going to yank down her top, see how far down the body glitter went, and hope it was edible. I needed to stop this now.

"My turn," I said.

2 /
reese

B randon tasted better than he should. It was taking all my restraint to keep from moaning against his mouth, and I was the one doing the kissing.

"My turn." He pressed a hand to my throat, his thumb applying just enough pressure to tempt. He backed me into the nearest wall, shifting the control of the kiss, and swallowed my gasp.

The longer he explored my mouth, the deeper he plunged his tongue and the harder he gripped my neck, the more my thoughts swam and blurred. This was... Things weren't supposed to be this way with Brandon. With my ex's boyfriend. Not like this. It was bad enough I still got butterflies around Danny, but I'd learned to ignore those.

Brandon crushed his body to mine, his erection digging into my stomach. There was no way I could ignore how good, how intense, this was.

But I didn't have a choice.

I broke away, and nudged him back enough to try to catch my breath. "I already told Adrienne I'd play the game." My voice was breathier than I wanted, but I couldn't admit out loud that Brandon won. Not ever, but especially right now.

"I already told Danny I'd go Christmas shopping with you." Brandon's voice was lined with gravel.

"So really, I'm the winner here." Danny's tone was husky. The kind of deep and turned on I only let myself remember when I was dreaming or watching Brandon fuck him.

Was it hot in here? Hotter than under the stage lights? I needed to lose some clothes.

"I take it back," Brandon said with a growl. "Don't blow your band manager."

"I wasn't really considering it." Not that anyone had thought otherwise. Though goddess be damned if I wasn't considering dropping to my knees in front of Brandon and dragging his zipper down with my teeth. I needed to shake this lust off, and instead I was picturing next steps.

When I forced myself to look at Brandon, the desire that stared back burned me.

"The two of you aren't going to stop there, are you?" Danny asked.

It was a good thing I liked living life by the seat

of my pants. I grinned at Brandon. "I don't think we have an official winner yet."

"I don't think we do." He wrapped my hair around his hand, yanked my head back hard enough to make me grunt, and claimed my mouth again.

The rough control was incredible, but I wasn't letting Brandon stay in charge. I used my full body to nudge him back onto the edge of the bed, and straddled his legs as I stood over him, pressing in with another kiss.

Brandon dragged his mouth along my jaw to my ear, his breath hot against my skin. "But don't touch my boyfriend." The words were so low, they were only meant for me, and the possession sent a shiver down my spine that was tempered by envy.

I moved my mouth back to his. "Of course not," I murmured against his lips. I was reckless, but I wasn't stupid. Danny was off-limits.

It didn't take much prompting to get Brandon to scoot back on the bed. I crawled up his body, and he reached for me. I wasn't tall enough to pin his wrists above his head, so I pinned them to his chest instead while I leaned in to devour his mouth.

I ground my hips, relishing the friction of clothes on clothes as the seam of my jeans dug into my pussy, and his erection helped.

Brandon bit my bottom lip. "If you keep that up, my zipper is going to rub a hole in my dick."

"So not sexy." I let him go and straightened up.

He glided his hands up my sides, pushing my shirt out of the way in the process, and stripped the clothing over my head. "We'll have to find a way to get the mood back."

I was intently aware of Danny watching us, and I used my lust for Brandon to blanket the desire to have Danny join us. With Brandon it would be easy to remind myself this was just sex. He was hot as fuck, and I'd entertained my fair share of fantasies about him. About being with him. About being with Danny and him...

I could have one of those.

Brandon teased his palms up my stomach to cup my breasts. When he tilted his body up, I leaned in and pressed a nipple to his lips. He drew it into his mouth to lick and suck, while he moved his other hand to squeeze my ass. To tease along the inside of my thighs.

I slid down his body. "If you're that worried about your cock, I only see one solution."

"What's that?" Brandon sounded amused.

I dragged his zipper down and worked him free. His moan when I wrapped my hand around his shaft was intoxicating. "Kiss it better," I said. I licked around the head. When I took him in my mouth, the groan that tore from his chest was like a skilled touch running over every inch of my body.

Apparently I was going to blow him, and the

need that pulsed between my legs loved every minute of it. I licked and stroked and his hips bucked as he fucked my face. As his breathing grew more stuttered and shallow, I increased the pace.

"Reese." The way he grunted my name was delicious. "Stop. You're gonna make me come."

I looked up at him through my lashes. "That sounds like a challenge."

His laugh was strained. "I promise you it's not." He pulled me to him and crushed his mouth to mine again. "I want to fuck you." He growled between hungry kisses. "I want to feel what it's like to bury myself inside you, and I want to watch your face when you get off."

"*That* sounds like a challenge."

Brandon grinned. "I really like your definition of competition."

"Are we going to spend the night swapping witty repartee, or are clothes coming off?" Danny's question was playful.

When I'd watched the two of them in the past it was fun, but it wasn't the same as me being the one on display. Danny's gaze was a phantom compared to the reality of his touch, but his watching us amplified my need while I was tangled with Brandon.

I looked at Brandon, who shrugged in agreement, and we extracted ourselves from the mattress long enough to strip off our clothes.

The way he studied my nude form set my skin on fire, and almost made me feel shy. I'd seen him naked before, but the most he'd seen from me was a glimpse when I played with myself while I watched him fuck Danny.

"You look even better without clothes than I imagined."

Heat flooded me at the implication he'd pictured me like this.

Brandon grabbed a condom from his wallet. I snagged it from him, nudged him back onto the bed, and straddled him again. With Danny, Brandon was always in control, but I wasn't surrendering any more to him than I already had.

I rolled the condom on him, and moved in to glide my slick pussy along his cock. I used him to tease me rather than letting him penetrate me.

He gripped my hips, stopping me. "I think you missed parts of what I said."

"I hear everything you say to me." I raised myself, reached between my legs to grip his shaft, and guided him inside me.

His moan at the penetration mingled with Danny's, and reverberated over me.

Was Danny imagining sliding inside me? Goddess, I wanted to think so, as much as I shouldn't entertain the thought.

I sat straight up, burying Brandon deep, and I

rocked slowly. I knew men, and once I picked up the pace, he wouldn't last long.

He pressed his thumb to my clit to stroke and tease, and I cupped my tits. I pinched my nipples and rolled them between my fingers. There was more grinding than bouncing as I rode Brandon. Danny's grunts told me he was lost in jerking off to the in-person porn.

"Fuck. Make her come already," Danny muttered.

The simple request, combined with Brandon's insistent and skilled touch, pushed me into climax. I clenched around him, falling into pleasure.

As the orgasm edged off, Brandon moved his hands to my hips and thrust up hard and fast.

This was pounding. The hammering inside me pushed me into another wave of ecstasy. I closed my eyes and leaned my head back, letting the sensation consume me. Letting the sound of Danny's climax weave into my thoughts. Relishing Brandon's pause, and then resumed pounding as he came.

We finally slowed to a stop, and I lay my head on his chest. I wanted to be doing this with Danny, but it wasn't an option, so instead I let Brandon's heart hammer against my ear.

He softened as he slid out of me, and I rolled off him to one side.

I lay next to Brandon on my back, my thoughts wrapped in bliss as the cool air brushed my bare, damp skin. I hadn't given or gotten that good in… I didn't want to think about how long it had been.

Danny crawled on to the bed on Brandon's other side, and rested his head on Brandon's chest. Loneliness and jealousy whimpered inside.

I deserved so much worse than seeing the two of them together. After what I did to Danny, all those years ago, I was lucky to be back in his life at all. Let alone this close.

Knowing that didn't mean I could completely shut off the longing when I saw the two of them together like this.

A phone rang, shattering the still and saving me from choking on regret rather than enjoying the post-sex glow.

Danny groaned. "That's yours."

"I know." Brandon sat up, crawled to the edge of the bed, and left his bare ass on display as he fished for his pants. "Yeah." He answered.

He sank back onto his haunches, and his shoulders slumped. "Is he okay? … Yeah, okay… I'm not in town, but I'll be there as soon as I can. Give me a few hours."

My gut sank at his tone. We shared a few friends, and I hoped this wasn't about one of them, but something told me this was worse.

3 /
danny

I'd liked the way the night started to look up after a shitty end to playing a shitty venue. The call from the hospital about Brandon's brother shattered that, though. The person who called hadn't been able to give him any information beyond saying Adam wasn't in critical condition.

Brandon was all business as we shoved our things into the truck. "I'll drop you off at home," he said to Reese.

She shook her head. "If you're going to the hospital, go. I'll figure the rest out."

I squeezed Brandon's hand, we piled into the SUV, and we were on our way. He was focused as we headed down the dark road.

Despite having a couple hour drive ahead of us, it was going to be tension filled and definitely not the right time to discuss what just happened between them. Between all of us. For all I knew, neither Brandon nor Reese *wanted* to talk about it.

And I shouldn't be dwelling on it, given the atmosphere in the car. But with no one talking, my mind was free to do what it wanted.

Reese and Brandon loved putting on a show— outside the bedroom and in it. A few years ago, Reese and I had moved beyond most of the mistrust and Brandon started coming on these mini road trips with us. It only took a few nights of sharing a room with her to realize the buzz that came with performing was intoxicating.

With a little—okay a lot of—negotiation, the three of us agreed it was pretty fucking hot to have her in the room while Brandon and I were screwing. For him it was the being watched. For me it was knowing they were both getting off on it.

I wasn't oblivious to their attraction to each other. The glances and the murmurs of appreciation when one of them thought the other wasn't paying attention were pretty obvious. And watching them together tonight... Should I have been jealous? I wasn't.

Brandon was the center of my universe. I loved him so very much, not only for saving me, but as the man who made me feel complete.

I glanced at Reese's reflection in the side mirror. She was sitting with her head pressed to the glass, staring blankly ahead. Each time we passed under a light, it bathed her in a yellow gray.

Even with the mood in the car, they both took my breath away. Even with how much I ached when Reese left me, so many years ago... But I knew she'd done it for reasons other than what she'd said, and that she regretted it, and she'd done a lot of soul searching and atoning to be back this close in my life. In our lives.

Seeing her with Brandon tonight sparked something I thought had died a long time ago. A dangerous, tempting urge that carried a deceptively simple question: could I have them both?

It felt wrong to vocalize that thought, despite me being the only person who heard it, especially right now. Brandon was worried about his brother and I was wondering if I could be fucking both him and the woman who nearly crushed my soul.

Knowing it was messed up didn't stop the thought from haunting me the entire drive. The images of the two of them together, and wondering if that could become a regular thing, were going to be with me for a while.

When we reached the hospital, Adam was in the ER waiting room. He was wearing scrubs, and had a lumpy plastic bag on the seat next to him.

"Thank God," Brandon muttered, and his shoulders slumped.

Adam gave us a sheepish grin. He was thirty-two, only about eight years younger than Brandon, but sometimes he still looked like he was barely an adult. Did Brandon look that young when I met him? Younger, even. But I doubted he'd ever looked that carefree.

"I didn't mean for you to bring the whole party." Adam's laugh ended in a hacking cough. "Sorry. Smoke inhalation. I promise I'm not contagious."

Brandon scrubbed his face and sat next to him. "What happened?"

"There was a fire in the workshop. It's toast. Which sucks because I was working on some amazing stuff." Some of Adam's levity vanished. "But I'll live. Too much smoke, and a few bruises. And the apartment I was staying in above the place is hosed. Get it? Fire? Hose." His laugh was weak.

I could practically hear Brandon thinking *not again*. He loved his brother, but Adam was more about the big ideas and less about what came after he had them. This was a new level of seriousness though; he'd built the workshop with a business partner, and they had a solid plan. Which I assumed wouldn't happen now.

Not that I thought the fire was his fault. He looked pretty bummed-slash-stressed about the entire event, as opposed to relieved to be out from under a project he was no longer interested in.

We dropped Reese at her apartment, but she didn't have room for most of her gear here, so I kept it at Brandon's and my place. Adam came back to the house with us, and I told him to leave the bag with his smoky clothes on the back porch to air out. He could wash everything in the morning. He needed to figure out what to do next, so he was staying in the guest room.

Which really he stayed in often enough it was like his second room.

"I promise I won't be here long. Just a few days. I appreciate it," Adam said.

I gave him a smile. "You know it's always fine." As he vanished into the room and closed the door behind him, I squeezed Brandon's hand. "Come to bed." He had to be drained. I still wanted to have the Reese conversation, but it might need to wait until morning.

Brandon kissed me on the cheek. "I have a tune in my head. I'll be up in a little bit."

I couldn't argue that. He'd been struggling with being blocked for a while, and if he was inspired, good for him.

The next morning, when I woke up to sunlight streaming in my eyes, I was surprised to be the only one in bed, with no indication Brandon had been here. I rubbed the sleep from my eyes, started the coffee maker as I walked through the kitchen, and headed into the basement.

We had a soundproof studio down here for recording, rehearsing, whatever we needed.

Brandon was sitting at the electric keyboard, headphones on and gaze fixed on the laptop screen on the table next to him.

When I touched him on the shoulder, he jumped.

Brandon spun in the chair to face me, dark circles under his wide eyes, and a grin plastered on his face. "You have to hear this." He pulled off his earphones and fitted them over my ears. "You set?" His voice was distant and muffled by the sound suppression.

I nodded, and he pressed *Play* on the laptop. The music started smooth and sweet. A simple keyboard tune that tugged at my heart. It slid into a rough, fast tempo that gripped me by the balls and didn't let go for the next four minutes.

When it was done, silence rang in my thoughts. I dropped the headphones around my neck and stared at him.

"Well?" he asked.

"Holy shit."

Brandon's wild grin grew. "Right?"

It was raw. It was nothing like what he usually did. But, "it's incredible."

"It was like I was possessed." His leg bounced while he talked. "It just came to me. I haven't felt like that in a long time. *Fuck* that felt good."

I understood the feeling. "You still working?"

"I should, um, coffee or something."

"I already started the pot." I pulled him to his feet, and we headed upstairs.

By the time we reached the kitchen, some of his nervous energy had evaporated, and he melted into a chair at the kitchen table.

"You should skip the coffee and get some sleep," I said.

Brandon frowned, then sighed. "Yeah. I am kind of tired." He stood again, and paused in front of me. "Last night at the hotel?"

"Yeah?" I both did and didn't want to hear what came next, especially with him coming down from creative high.

He brushed his lips over mine. "Hot as fuck, exactly the way it looked. And it's not going to happen again."

"Okay." I pointed him toward the bedroom and gave him a push to propel him forward.

After Brandon vanished into our room, I took the seat he'd just been in, adopting a similar slumped posture. I should be satisfied, pleased even, with his assurance. But it wasn't what I wanted to hear.

What was wrong with me that I wanted what happened between Brandon and Reese to happen again?

4 /
brandon

Danny nudged me awake with a kiss. There was more nudging than kissing, but it still wasn't a bad way to greet consciousness. "We have to be at Dustin's in less than an hour. Do you want to get up now, or snooze until the last minute and leave in a panicked rush?" he said.

It was a question worth giving some serious consideration to. I hadn't pulled an all-nighter in years, and a day later, I still felt the effects. I also still felt the buzz from what I'd created, and that had me hopped up despite the exhaustion.

"I'm up." I pushed myself out of bed.

I sleep-walked my way through a shower and getting dressed, hoping to hold onto the pleasant fuzzy feeling as long as possible. Traces of a dream lingered in my thoughts. A replay of Friday night with Reese. In my dream, details changed, new scenarios appeared, but it was all nearly as scorching as the reality. I hated to say that my musical inspiration was related, but…

Taking that risk with her was a rush I couldn't compare to anything else. I needed more freedom like that. Maybe not *exactly* of the fucking someone else variety. Unless it was Reese again. But no, definitely not. That was a bad idea.

Something that got my adrenaline racing though, and let me shrug off responsibility for short blinks of time.

I headed into the kitchen, and was surprised to find Adam already up, and making phone calls. I was used to seeing him move from one project to the next without flinching. This time though, he'd been working since yesterday to try to find out what was salvageable in his workshop and where else he could go to get back to work.

He'd also been struggling to get a hold of his business partner.

Sure, it hadn't even been two days, but this was a long time for him to hold on.

I grabbed Adam's attention with a silent snap.

"Can you hang on a minute," he said to the person on the other end of the phone. He covered the mouthpiece. "What's up?"

"We're heading out. Probably back this afternoon. Want me to pick you anything up?"

Adam gave me a tight smile. "Two months of lost work and maybe a new 3D printer?"

Poor guy. "I'll ask around about the printer."

"Thanks." He went back to his call.

"Heads-up." Danny's voice drew my attention.

Without thinking, I put my hand in the air and snagged the keys he tossed me. He handed me a to-go mug of coffee as we headed outside.

I took a sip of a drink almost hot enough to scorch the roof of my mouth. Perfect. "God, I love you."

"*Duh*." He grinned.

The music was loud and the conversation limited on the drive across town. When we got to Dustin's, Reese's Jeep was already parked out front. The purple Willys Jeep had been a graduation present from her mother more than twenty years ago. The two of them had kept it running together until her mother passed away when Reese was in her mid-twenties, and since then Reese poured her soul into making sure the Jeep lived on.

She was seated on the front porch, chin in her hands, and looking very different from Friday night. The stage makeup was gone, she was wearing a battered old sweatshirt with Danny's alma matter on it over faded jeans.

"Where's the man of the hour?" I asked as we joined her on the steps.

She shrugged. "Your guess is as good as mine. Who moves at the end of November anyway?"

"The guy who's tired of paying for a house he's not living in," Danny said.

Reese rolled her eyes. "Whatever. Stupid reasonable reason is reasonable."

Dustin was our Director of Marketing for the game company I worked at, AcesPlayed. He had also been dating two co-workers for the last several months.

Speaking of, there were two of them now. Phillip parked his SUV behind mine. "Sorry," he called as he and Adrienne headed toward us. "There was some confusion with our reservation at the truck rental place."

"I told them, if they'd gotten the truck last night and we slept here…" Adrienne trailed off.

It made me wish *I'd* chosen the sleep in option, but I never saw them late to anything, so I could forgive it this once. "I'm not saying anything. I'm just glad someone's tapping that ass." I gave them an appreciative look.

"Excuse me?" Adrienne's offense sounded fake.

"What? I meant his." I jerked a thumb at Phillip.

Adrienne pursed her lips. "So did I. I can wear a strap-on as well as the next girl."

"*Nice.*" Reese gave her a high five.

The dynamic in our small group of friends changed when Adrienne started dating Dustin and Phillip. Not in a bad way, but in an obvious way.

Then again, the dynamic had changed years ago, when Dustin started working with us. When Reese came back into Danny's life. When I met Danny.

Had I really known Phillip for twenty years? We met when we started working at a tiny little gaming company no one had ever heard of. That had gotten big, been swallowed by a larger company, and started over again.

Rinslet was big again, but we'd left five years ago to start this new and risky thing. A massively multi-player online role-playing game with adult content. Not just swearing and violence, but sex. The characters could get naked. They could fuck anyone in game, multiple people at once, whatever.

The game was in open beta now, and working with the content we did required a certain level of comfort with sexuality. Considering way back when we were young and reckless and horny, at that first tiny company, a lot of us unwound by fucking everyone else in the office, it wasn't a hard transition to make. Those of us who were originals joked sometimes that we'd just brought our old orgy culture to the game, and stuck it in a magical cyberpunk society.

"And there's the man of the hour." Danny's comment and pointing drew my attention to the end of the street. "Making a late entrance to the pleasure and surprise of the crowds."

Dustin backed the moving van into the driveway. When he stepped out, everyone applauded. He bowed. "If I knew bringing donuts and coffee would get me this kind of reception, I'd do it all the time."

"How did you *not* know that?" I stared at him in disbelief.

"You stopped for donuts when you were already late?" Phillip asked.

Reese clapped. "You brought sugar?"

"Yes to all of the above." Dustin looked at Phillip and shrugged. "What? I wanted some. I brought enough for everyone."

Danny was already opening the passenger door of the truck and grabbing one of the drink holders. "Dibs on cream-filled."

Adrienne snorted.

Dustin pulled a donut box off the seat. "I brought enough cream filling for everyone who wants it too."

"TMI. Seriously." Reese scoffed.

Dustin opened the box for her. "They had pink frosted."

Her scowl vanished and she clapped twice. "You *do* love me."

We all grabbed our donuts and coffee—Dustin knew our orders, including who would be on their second cup—and followed him into the house. He'd already moved out most of the smaller, personal stuff. Some of his furniture sold with the house, most was going into storage for now, and the rest would go to Phillip's.

Or Dustin's new place. Or whatever the proper terminology was. Dustin had already sorted everything, so he pointed out what went where, and we got to work.

There wasn't a lot of conversation as we loaded the things for Phillip's into his SUV, mine, and Reese's jeep. The storage stuff went into the moving van.

The whole thing had the potential to be a clusterfuck of a disaster, especially when we got to Phillip's and had to swap out some of his furniture for the new. But Dustin was a master at planning events, including a moving day, and things went smoothly.

Once cars were unloaded and more was put into the moving truck, Phillip, Addie, and Reese stayed at the house to do more sorting and rearranging. Danny and I followed Dustin to his storage unit to help him unload the truck and give him a ride back after he returned it.

Dustin was in the front passenger seat and Danny in the second row as we drove back to the new place.

"How'd the show go?" Dustin asked.

And now the memories of what happened after were back. I did not need a hardon right now. He was mostly asking if the booking was any better than normal, though. He and his partners were familiar with the bad contract situation, and they made it to about ninety percent of the shows. They'd only shrugged off the chance this time because Thursday was Thanksgiving with Dustin's sister and nieces, and Friday was with Adrienne's brother and his partners.

I was glad we didn't deal with those kinds of holiday schedules. Danny's parents were in Florida and didn't expect their adult son to visit every holiday, and my father took his own life a few years ago. Adam did his own thing.

"Show-wise, bottom end of the spectrum, but not the worst." Danny answered Dustin's question. "What came after though…"

There was no way he was bringing that up. I tried to grab his attention in the rearview mirror, to give him a stern *shut up* look, but he wasn't watching me.

"There was a fire in Adam's workshop," Danny said. "He thinks he lost almost everything."

Right. That.

Dustin frowned. "That sucks. Tell him to hit us up if we can help."

"If you know anyone selling an inexpensive but solid 3D printer…" I put the request out there.

"I'll let you know what I hear."

When we got back to Phillip's—everyone's—place, we ordered pizza. The six of us were sitting around talking and unwinding, when multiple phones chimed within seconds of each other.

Everyone reached for their pockets or purses, but the messages were for Phillip, Dustin, and me. The text was from Judith, our boss and owner of the company we worked for. Luna, our cybersecurity expert, and Elliot, our Director of Development were copied on the message too. Basically, the bulk of management.

The note was simple in its threat. It contained a link to a crowdfunding site and the note *Get this down now. Then tell me how it happened.*

I shared a glance with Phillip as Dustin read the message aloud.

"So, what is *this?*" Adrienne asked.

I clicked the link Judith sent, but my gut was already sinking. The campaign was for, as it said, *a hot new MMORPG like you've never seen before.* I recognized the thumbnail in the video as currently unreleased art from our game, and when the music started playing—music I'd only just finalized a week or two ago that was on our servers but wouldn't be shown to the world until RinCon—my gut sank.

"We were hacked," Phillip said. "And someone's trying to claim our demo for RinCon is their game."

"It was funded in under an hour of go-live." Dustin didn't look up from his phone.

Danny pressed his head next to mine to see the screen. "Duh. You guys are the best."

That was true, but this was still bad. It was easy enough to get the campaign taken down; finding out how someone got a hold of our demo was a bigger concern.

Adrienne's phone rang. "It's Luna."

"Call Elliot," I said to Phillip at the same time he said, "Calling Elliot."

Adrienne answered her phone.

Any plans I had for the rest of my day were gone. I'd need to be in contact with the rest of the group, and since more than half of us were in this room, it made sense for me to stay here. I turned to Danny.

"I'll bring you your laptop," Danny said before I could vocalize the thought. "Reese?"

"Yeah, you can get a lift." Reese blew the room a kiss. "Call me if you need takeout or anything, and I'll be here."

Danny squeezed my hand and brushed his lips over mine. "Be back soon."

"Thanks." And in the meantime, I'd hope we were on the *at least they used lube* end of the fucked scale, rather than the *they went in dry with both fists* end.

5 /
reese

"Hold up." Brandon's call brought Danny and me to a stop. As we reached my Jeep. Brandon jogged up to join us. "You owe me a game, Reese."

He was really pushing this now? Not that I minded, since the question brought back memories of the bet that led to it. *Fuck*. That kiss. That fucking.

He stepped close enough I could smell his cologne mixed with the faint scent of a day of hard labor. That was way more tempting than it should be.

"Unless you'd like to go for double or nothing." Brandon's tone was light, and a smile tugged up one corner of his mouth, but that didn't stop me from being tempted.

I forced myself to take a step back. "We both already admitted we were in. Double of nothing is nothing. Fix your shit, and I'll get online when the timing is better."

Brandon shrugged, and turned to Danny. "If you think you can help, bring your machine too. That is, if you're interested."

In a former life, he'd been in cybersecurity like Luna. It was my understanding that she was a master at keeping people out of systems—though apparently not that good—but Danny was a genius at finding out who had already been in a system.

"I'm interested in seeing this shut down," Danny said.

Brandon pulled Danny in for a long kiss, I felt it in my toes.

"See you soon." Brandon turned and headed inside.

Danny and I climbed into my Jeep and I headed toward his and Brandon's place. The silence was weird, but the last few days hadn't exactly been normal.

"Are we okay?" I glanced sideways at him with the question, to get a gauge of his first reaction.

He twisted his mouth, but he didn't look surprised or upset. "Should we not be?"

"I mean, I slept with your boyfriend."

"Pft." Danny waved a hand. "I do that all the time."

A laugh slipped out, carried on half-amusement, half-nervousness. "Because he's *your* boyfriend. And before you say it, I know you agreed before, but after it happens, feelings can change." Like mine. Like me wanting to do it again. And maybe again. And maybe with Danny joining in.

I shut the thought down.

Danny squeezed my knee. "We're good. I promise." The assurance was genuine.

How did I feel about that? I wanted him more now. We used to be so good together. *Used to be*—I needed to remember that because I didn't deserve Danny.

"I'm guessing we're not on for tonight," I needed to change the subject. Christmas was my favorite holiday, and Danny usually helped me decorate my apartment. This year, we'd even convinced Brandon to help.

Danny winced. "I don't know yet, but it's my goal."

"In that case, I won't fill your slot," I teased.

He grinned. "You'd better not."

I dropped him off at home, and he promised to give me a call in a few hours and let me know if decorating was still on.

I headed to my apartment. The studio used to be a mother-in-law apartment for the house above me, and the landlord rented it out as a separate house now. It was tiny, but it was clean and the family upstairs was quiet and this was home.

Inside, I kicked off my shoes, pulled my hair

into a messy bun, and fitted my earbuds in place, to prep for my first call.

In my mother's last days, she was in the hospice portion of a publicly funded nursing home. We couldn't afford more. The other residents in both halves of the facility were twenty, thirty, even forty years older than she was.

And so many of them just wanted someone to talk to. I'd visit mom, and if she was asleep, or I was waiting for the staff to be done treating her, I'd go hang out with the other residents.

These days I worked for a service that offered check-in calls with seniors. I'd call my clients and we'd chat, usually far longer than we were supposed to. I hated that I was supposed to bill people by the hour for a conversation, and I rarely billed more than the minimum.

I grabbed a soda from the fridge—it was a good thing I didn't keep beer in the house—and dialed my appointment.

"Hey, darlin'," Bambi answered.

I didn't know what name she'd been given at birth, but she'd changed it legally when she was eighteen, because she was going to be a star. She had more or less adopted me a few years ago, and she was one of my favorite clients to talk to.

"Hey. How are you? How was your Thanksgiving?" She'd had big plans with her girlfriends.

"Too adult for your virgin ears."

I laughed. "Okay. Whatever." This was good. It would take my mind off the incredible sex from a few days ago.

"Trust me, Buttercup, you don't want to hear about a bunch of old ladies sitting around talking about the dragon dildo website Sofie's granddaughter sent her."

Now I was laughing harder. "First of all, you're not old, and second, I hope to be that person when I'm your age."

Bambi snorted. "By the time you're my age, science will have turned those... what are they called... deep throat images into printable images, and you'll never age again."

"Deep throat?" I tossed the word in my head, looking for any connection that matched the context of her reply. "Deep fake?"

"Don't correct me, young lady. I know what I said. There's no way those women are actually swallowing those cocks."

"It's all about controlling your gag reflex, and yes I know from experience."

Bambi gave an exaggerated cough, as if clearing her throat. "Don't brag, it's not becoming. And don't correct your elders."

We chatted until I had to let her go for my next appointment. I talked to two more clients over the next three hours, and then it was time to get ready for decorating with Danny and Brandon.

Thinking about seeing Danny and Brandon again... Who was I? I didn't get hung up on shit like that. Had it really been that long since I had incredible sex with someone other than my vibrator?

That must be my hang-up—my revisiting the moment over and over wasn't the who, it was the what. I'd find a good orgasm or two somewhere else, and I'd be fine again. And as long as Danny was free tonight, hanging out with the guy who had been my best friend for ages wouldn't be awkward at all.

I washed off the stink from the moving we did this morning, but didn't bother with makeup or doing my hair. This was decorating my home, and no one else would see me. No one to impress.

Regardless of what the tiny little girl in the back of my head, who had loved Danny since we were kids, was screaming.

Outside my window, snow was starting to fall. It didn't seem likely Danny and Brandon would make it over tonight, but I had to call anyway. As I grabbed my phone and dialed Danny, I turned to watch a few white flakes turn into a heavy curtain. I listened to several rings before Danny answered, breathless. "Hey."

"Decorating?"

"What? Oh. Fuck. I'm sorry Reese, I got so caught up in this thing, I lost track of time."

What? Danny didn't do that. He had, once upon

a time when it was his job, but not anymore. "No worries." I made sure I sounded like I meant it. His getting hung up was expected, after all. "I'll see you for practice tomorrow night?"

"Yeah, definitely. I'm sorry."

I forced myself to smile, so the look would shine through in my voice. "Seriously, it's okay. How's everything going?"

"Eh. Not as bad as it could be, but not as good as we'd like. Hey, I need to get back to it. Catch up with you tomorrow?"

"Sure. Talk to you then." I was pretty sure he hung up before I finished talking. Was I hurt that he couldn't make time for tonight? Of course. I had a hard time blaming him, though. He was doing something he loved, with someone he loved.

I needed a boost of good cheer, and there was no reason I couldn't decorate by myself. There wasn't enough room in here for much, but I had a foot-high Christmas tree, with tiny ornaments and the littlest string of lights to adorn it.

I turned on the Christmas music, and sang along as I got to work.

When I was little, Christmas was my favorite holiday. Other people hated being Christmas babies, but I loved it. We never had much money growing up, but Mom decorated every December. The house would be lights and color and amazing, and then there was that one day a year—my birthday—when

I'd wake up and there would be a present for me under the tree and a small pile of candy.

We weren't religious, so I didn't understand the significance of the day to other people. I assumed Mom was doing it all to celebrate me, and I loved it. I figured out as I got older, went to school, listened to the other kids talk, that our Christmas was nothing compared to theirs, and the way Mom did things meant only one present for both birthday and Christmas. I didn't care. By then I already knew that we decorated the house, people decorated the mall, everyone around the world bought presents for their loved ones, because it was my birthday.

Ah, to be young and that kind of arrogant again.

I still loved the holiday, and the good it brought out in people, though.

It didn't take me long to put everything up. I'd never found a small enough tree-topper that was appropriate for me, but I would. When I reached the bottom of the box, a smaller box sat at the bottom, taunting me.

It would stay there, the way it did every year. With the snow blanketing the ground outside, and the music having stopped in the background, a somber mood sank in. "I miss you, Mom." I blew the tree a kiss, and settled onto the mattress to read and distract myself from the loneliness.

6 /
danny

W̲e'd turned Phillip's living room into a war room. Dustin and Brandon had spent the entire afternoon scouring for any traces of the stolen and leaked content, and getting it taken down. That didn't mean it was gone—once people realized it was from an existing game, we expected new copies would pop up.

Luna and Elliot were represented by the two phones sitting between us. Once Elliot confirmed no code got out, only music and images, he'd started helping us dissect the video.

The stress in the air was tangible, and I loved it anyway. I retired from this kind of work years ago, because the clients were unpredictable and the demand added to my drinking problem. But the problem solving… I could do this all the time.

When my phone rang, I jumped. Reese's name flashed on the screen, and my heart sank. "Hey." I answered, giving her most of my attention, but keeping a sliver on my work.

None of the pieces we'd looked at so far had their original headers. Which made sense. The person doing this knew enough to strip out the information that said where the video came from, so that it looked like it was theirs.

"Decorating?" she asked.

"Fuck. I'm sorry Reese, I got so caught up in this thing, I lost track of time." There had to be something hidden in this file that said who it came from, though.

"No worries." Her disappointment was masked under false cheer. After knowing her for years, it was easy to hear. "I'll see you for practice tomorrow night?"

"Yeah, definitely. I'm sorry." There was one place, and as I dug into the audio, I wasn't sure if I wanted to find what I was looking for or not. Not a lot of people knew how to stash information here, but Brandon was one of them, because I taught him.

"Seriously, it's okay. How's everything going?" Reese asked.

"Eh. Not as bad as it could be, but not as good as we'd like. Hey, I need to get back to it. Catch up with you tomorrow?"

"Sure. Talk to you th—"

I disconnected before she finished, and winced

with guilt. But I found an answer to our leaked information issue. Or at least a hint. A tucked away piece of metadata with our home IP address on it. "Fuck." The exclamation slipped out, and everyone in the room stared at me.

"I found something." Luna's voice came from the phone closest to me. "Is it the same thing you found?"

I hoped not. Could I pretend I didn't know what this was? Not the best idea if we wanted a solution. "Don't know. Is it?" These audio files came from our network, and it was very possible the images did too. Brandon kept a lot of work on his personal machine. AcesPlayed hadn't been hacked, we had.

"Before we go back and forth too much," Luna said, "I'll point out that I have a whitelist of IP addresses for employees who access the network from home, and I can tell who this belongs to."

I sucked in a sharp breath through my teeth. "Yeah. We found the same thing."

"And you were going to blame poor, innocent me for not doing my job." Luna's tone was light.

This hardly seemed like the time to point out that she was a lot of things, but I doubted innocent was one of them. "I had no intention of saying such a thing."

"You were thinking it."

Busted.

"That's okay, I was too." Luna sounded more

relieved than upset. "I can't get anything else from it, do you think you can?"

"I'll have to dig, but I'll try."

"What does this mean for us?" Brandon's question shattered the eerie feeling of no one else talking.

Luna's exhale was loud. "If you have a computer with AcesPlayed assets on it, disconnect it now. From the internet, from the network, from your phones. Turn the Wi-Fi off completely."

Groans echoed through the room. I'd never heard a group of people more disappointed that they'd been told not to work on a weekend. Though to be fair, this was more limiting.

"Personal machines in the office tomorrow. I'll make sure you're all locked down and then you can surrender your nights to work again. I'll tell the rest of the office," Luna said.

Which left me with the only internet capable computer in the room, and a problem I still didn't have the answer to. "I'm going to keep digging."

"I'll do the same. Let me know what you find." Luna hung up.

Phillip picked up his phone from the coffee table. "That means we're all off the hook. See you tomorrow, Elliot."

"Yeah, let me know," Elliot said.

Brandon and I said our goodbyes and headed into the stormy weather. The snow had stopped falling, and the plows had already been out, leaving the roads clear, but the landscape blanketed in silence.

We stopped next to our vehicles, and Brandon squeezed my hand. "See you at home?"

"If I'm a few minutes late, don't call the cops. I need to stop by Reese's."

His frown melted into understanding. "The thing?"

"The thing."

He gave me a quick kiss, and we were on our way, driving in the same direction until I hit the intersection that took me on a different path. Driving after a snowfall, when no one had been out to disturb the world, was an experience in eerie beauty. I loved the way the lights reflected off both the ground and the clouds in the sky, wrapping the world in a bubble of pale yellow.

I got to Reese's, grabbed the present off the seat, and gingerly walked the unshoveled path up to her door.

She answered with a smile that didn't hide a faint sadness in her eyes. "Were you really working this late?"

"And I'll probably do more when I get home. I want to find this person. But first, I had to come find you." I handed her the gift.

"It's not Christmas."

"You should open it anyway." A glance past her

told me she'd already done the decorating, but it wasn't too late to add one more piece.

She gave me a suspicious look, then tore off the colorful paper. When she saw the box inside, she managed a smile and a gasp simultaneously. She pulled out the winged girl in a crop top and jeans, who was playing a guitar. "You got me a new angel for my tree. Where did you..."

"I asked Adam to make it for me." I'd given him the specs and pointed him toward a bunch of reference photos, and he'd 3D printed it, then painted it.

"It's amazing and perfect and I love it. Thank you." Reese threw her arms around my neck.

I squeezed back, and a pulse of desire surged inside. To hold her longer. To push her inside and steal a kiss. To do more. Instead, I forced myself to let go. "I need to take off before the snow starts again."

"I agree." Some of her sadness leaked back. "See you tomorrow."

———

Brandon was already gone when I woke up. Judging by the numbers on the clock, he'd probably been at work for a couple of hours.

I hated that I hadn't found my answers yesterday, and even more than the leak basically happened on my watch. I wanted to get back to it today, but I'd exhausted all avenues I could think of for searching, the hole was patched, and I had to get to my own job.

I ran on autopilot through getting ready, and sighed at the sight of an empty coffee pot. The second mug in the sink implied Adam may be responsible for my lack of morning caffeination.

It was my day to grab coffee and donuts for the first meeting of the day anyway. There had been a lot of discussion—way too much in my opinion—about whether or not it was a good idea to provide coffee for teenagers.

Those of us in the *I'll allow it* camp argued that since this was an addiction recovery group for kids whose parents had kicked them out of their houses for being something other than straight or cis, that giving them coffee was the least of their concerns for their future.

My order was ready for me when I got to Loading Java, and Lyn grabbed me the biggest coffee they sold while Violet and I loaded everything into the passenger seat of my car.

Brandon and everyone he worked with had been coming here for a while, since it was across their street from their offices, but when Luna introduced me to Violet, I thought my prayers had been answered.

Not the same way they were when I met Brandon, but I'd been feeling a bit of discontent for a while, and feeling guilty on top of that. What did I have to be unhappy with? Perfect boyfriend, perfect life, perfectly flawed best friend and bandmate... But something was missing.

I thanked Violet, told her I'd see her in a few hours, and waved to Brandon's building. He was in meetings all day, so I wouldn't see him while I was here. Then I was on my way.

Violet not only managed Loading Java for Lyn, but volunteered at the shelter for LGBTQ+ teens that I was heading to. When I started talking to her, months ago, she mentioned they needed someone to run some of their addiction recovery groups for older teens.

I'd been sober for almost a decade, knew my way around an AA meeting, and felt for these kids who needed someone who cared, so I stepped in.

I remembered being where these kids were, despite my being older when it happened to me. It was so long ago, but there were days when it still felt like yesterday. I'd been dating Reese, we were singing in clubs and drawing a huge audience, and we were going to conquer the world with our music.

Then she lost her mother, and spiraled with the grief. We held onto each other, but she was struggling with the idea of losing someone she loved so much.

She got what she insisted was a better offer. From her current manager—live and learn—all she had to do was break up the band and kick off her solo career. She'd done it. She dumped me, she stopped performing with me. She cut off all contact with me.

Work started falling apart about the same time, and there was no doubt the two stresses fed each other. I'd moved into a bottle of whatever was cheap and had a high alcohol content, and lived there.

The memory didn't haunt me the way it used to, Reese had spent years earning my trust again after she came back into my life, and I knew she'd learned. But when I listened to these kids tell their stories, still in that rock bottom spot and thinking nothing in the world mattered but numbing the pain, I felt those ghosts of the past.

And now I was wondering what it would be like to let Reese further into my life again. To have her as part of my relationship with Brandon.

I was an idiot for even considering it, but every time the thought entered my head, it felt like a good idea. Even now, with those old wounds exposed and aching, I liked the thought of having more with Reese again, without losing Brandon.

7 /
brandon

The entire management team—which was also more than a third of the company—sat in one of our meeting rooms. Which was really like any of the other rooms in the AcesPlayed building, but with an oblong conference room table in the middle, instead of desks and computers and walls filled with each respective team's workflows.

Judith stood at the front of the room, her face pinched and her lips pursed. She was as bothered about needing to have this meeting as the rest of us were. "Do we need to send Luna to every person's house and make sure everything is secure?"

The question wasn't directed at me, but I was still furious that this happened because of some sort of flaw on my end.

"The patch I have for personal computers is solid," Luna said. "But each machine takes me a few hours to set up and test, and it's a lot of configuration, so I can't really start one then move on to the next. I'm going to be working on them for weeks."

"I'm not leaving my home computer here or offline for weeks." Elliot was saying what all of us were thinking.

Sonya, who was our Director of Story, raised her hand. Like everyone in the room except for Luna, who was younger, she was about forty. She'd come from Rinslet, like so many of us, but hadn't been with the company quite as long. She was outgoing in a very small group, but put her in a room full of people, and she went quiet.

Not that I had an issue with that. She was nice, and like all of us, she was one of the best at what she did.

"Sonya, yes." Judith called on her.

Sonya ducked her head when everyone turned in her direction. "Story can help Nigel with testing. Give us a checklist of what to look for."

"Nigel's not…" Luna clenched her jaw. Unhappy was odd for her, but she and Nigel clashed early on when she started working here, and they hadn't gotten past it. "I'd love to have help from Story. And QA if they're available."

"We are." Nigel wasn't a bad guy, but he did have the kind of attention to detail that was required from a director of Quality Assurance. "My entire team is available, if that will make things go faster."

Luna's smile was tight. "Looking forward to it. That cuts a little bit of time off my estimate, but I still have to do the installs. Can we bring Danny in?" She looked between Judith and me.

I'd rather we didn't. This kind of work added to his breakdown, years ago. But this was a short-term contract, with people I trusted to not demand too much, and, "It's not my decision."

"Wait. Danny. Pretty, plays guitar... Or are we talking about a different Danny?" Judith asked.

Luna nodded. "Same Danny. He helped last night. Kicks ass."

"He knows his shit," Elliot confirmed. "Not the way Luna does, but they might as well have been speaking Greek last night, for as well as I kept up."

Dustin stared at him. "You speak Greek."

"Enough ask where they sell the Ouzo, and to *askzaharoplastis itan o babas sou?*" Elliot said. "And I'm rusty."

If I remembered right, he'd told me once the line meant *was your father a pastry chef?* And that it was a pick-up line. He was also far more fluent than he claimed.

"Sorry to point out the elephant in the room." Nigel's tone implied he wasn't. "But if this happened on Brandon's network, it happened on Danny's as well. The point is to make our machines *more* secure. In fact, why are the rest of us paying the price for their shitty security?"

Maybe Nigel wasn't that great a guy after all. "Danny's specialty is finding people, and he'd be working with Luna's patch." I struggled to keep the frustration from my retort.

"Can he find this person?" Judith asked.

"Given enough time, yes." I had no doubt.

Judith clacked her nails on the table in front of her, the tapping echoing through the room. "Luna, make Danny an offer. Pay whatever his contract fee is, and see if you can bring Cole in too."

Luna clapped twice, and her grin was back. "Will do."

"The stolen assets." Judith moved on to the next topic without pause. "They're out there, the surprise is gone, they're associated with a different game, even though it's not one that will ever get off the ground, what do we do?"

"New assets to plug into the demo." Phillip made it sound so simple. His Art department was second in size only to Development, so it probably was easy for him.

I was a department of one, and I'd dragged the last piece out. My burnout snarled at the thought of having to do so again so soon, especially since we'd have to be finished ASAP for RinCon.

Judith looked at me. "Yes or no?"

Regardless of how my creativity felt, there was only one answer. Everyone in this room was here because we believed this game would be ground-breaking in as many ways as were possible, and that meant not skipping steps. "Agreed. New assets."

"Great." Judith stood. "Ivan will send out meeting notes. Make it all happen people."

The rest of us gathered up our laptops and tablets to get back to work.

"Brandon. Stick around for a minute." Judith's request stopped me.

She hadn't always been the big boss. She started on the bottom rung like I had at Rinslet. We'd been friends much longer than I'd worked for her.

Was this about the fact that the leaked demo came from my computer? That I'd been *hiding* my boyfriend's cybersecurity experience? I joined her at the front of the room, and we waited until we were the only people in the room.

"You okay?" She asked.

I hadn't expected that. "Fine. Why?"

"Because you looked like Phillip pissed in your Cheerios when he suggested replacement assets."

I tried to push out one of those casual, *it's nothing* laughs, but the sound came out strangled. "Lot on my mind. Nothing I can't handle."

She frowned.

"You ever wish you hadn't taken this all on?" I regretted the question as soon as I asked it, because I already knew the answer, and worse, I knew what my asking implied.

She shook her head. "No. Do you?"

"Absolutely not." It was true. I wanted to be part of this. I also wanted to shove past the drain I felt every time I tried to create.

Judith sighed. "You've got a new score to write. But I'm here to listen. I'll even stop being your boss for a few minutes if you ever want to talk."

"I'm good, but thanks." I gave her my broadest smile, and made myself mean it.

I headed back to the Sound and Music part of the building. This had been a satellite branch for a community college, but when they moved their business school mostly online, they got rid of the physical location. Judith had picked the property up cheap.

Each team had one or more classrooms that they'd set up however was best for what they were doing. As a team of one, I had a room all to myself, but that didn't mean I was rambling around in empty space. A tiny recording studio, with all the soundproofing and acoustics, occupied the office attached to the room. In the main area, there was an electric keyboard, an upright piano, several instruments, and other assorted tools for making sounds.

I could be using stock noises, but some things just sounded better when I recreated them myself.

Though, they didn't sound like anything when I couldn't focus on what to create. I sat at my computer desk and stared at the screen, willing inspiration to strike.

I didn't realize I'd been doing so for almost an hour until Luna set my personal laptop next to me, startling me.

"You're clean," she said.

I spun in my chair to find she'd made herself comfortable on the taller seat next to the electric keyboard.

"What did you find?" I asked.

She hooked her heels on the rungs and twisted back and forth. "Nothing. You're clean, as in, no one's been on that computer who wasn't authorized. There's no sign of forced entry. So whoever did it had your password or one of their own."

"So…"

"Do I need to lecture you on being more cautious with your login information?"

I stared at her, lips pursed and jaw clenched, letting my expression convey my response.

"That's what I thought." Luna grinned and hopped to her feet. "I set you up with the new security anyway. We might as well do this while everyone's paranoid. Ask Danny if he's up for helping?"

"Yeah. I'll do that, but I can guarantee it won't be until at least tomorrow. He's booked today."

"That's okay. Cole will be here after lunch to help me get started. Back to the salt mines." Luna half skipped out of the room.

Ah, to be a decade younger and have that much energy and enthusiasm.

I emailed Luna's job offer to Danny rather than texting or calling, so as not to disturb his work. I was surprised when he replied within a few minutes, and more surprised when he said he was in. At least it meant having him in the office with me for a few days. That would be nice.

The rest of the workday was business as usual. I willed myself to come up with new music for the upcoming event, Sonya and Jeremy sent me their revised script for a different project, and I plucked out a few chords for that, before giving up on all of it.

Maybe something would come to me on the way home or in the shower in the morning or maybe I could summon a muse or a demon. Would I sell my soul to get my job done? Reese had negotiated with someone far worse than a demon, and while she hadn't offered her soul, it was close. She was miserable.

So no, I wouldn't sell my soul for inspiration. Probably. Maybe. I'd need a little something extra to sweeten the deal.

When I got home, Adam was nowhere to be found. With any luck, he was making headway in whatever he was doing that he'd been tight-lipped about up until now.

The light on the doorway at the foot of the

basement was on, meaning Danny and Reese were in the music room. The room was mostly sound-proof, but if Reese was drumming, or they were really into a song, I'd hear something out here, and I didn't.

I pressed a button near the door, that was a sort of doorbell. It would flash a similar light inside the room, letting them know someone was waiting to be let in. The LED light changed colors depending on whether the request was coming from here or the front door.

A moment later, Danny unlocked the door. "Hey. Welcome home." He gave me a quick kiss.

"We need your opinion." Reese was seated behind him at the drums.

The room took up the entirety of the basement, but given we'd crammed almost as much in here as I had at work—no upright piano and I made Reese leave the big drums in storage—it was a tight space.

I stood near the door. "Do you want praise or honesty?" Important question to ask up front.

She gave me a look that said *duh*. "I assume it'll be both. But honesty would be nice."

Danny settled on a tall stool, and grabbed his favorite acoustic guitar. Odd for their sound, but not unheard of when Reese was trying to figure out why she didn't like a tune. Something I could sympathize with more than ever today.

She counted off a three-four beat with a combination of snare drum and the occasional bass drum hit.

Both sounds were low enough that it was easy to hear her when she started talking. "Picture this. Cinderella at the masquerade."

Danny slid into an ascending series of chords that carried apprehension mixed with excitement.

"She makes her grand entrance, and all eyes are on her." Reese's words were the perfect compliment to what Danny was playing. "Everyone wants to know who she is, suitor after suitor asks her to dance, including the prince."

The tension faded from the music, blossoming into excitement. Thrill. Joy.

"She's never had so much praise. No one has ever noticed her like this before. It's intoxicating," Reese said. "Cinderella finds herself in the arms of the prince more often than not, and she loses herself in the evening."

The song was achingly bright, almost too much. The story was good. Not unique, but a nice touch. It would be fun to see what kind of lyrics Danny put to this once he dug into it.

"She doesn't hear the first ten chimes of the clock. By the time the eleventh strikes, she's tearing away, running for the exit. But strike twelve happens while she's still in the middle of the ballroom." Reese's tone dropped toward sadness along with the music.

"Her fairy godmother's spell vanishes, and she's left herself, in tattered rags, amid all the town's elite." The song glided into somber, and so did Reese's voice. "Everyone's still asking who she is, but the questions are now disgust, instead of awe. Until the prince's best friend steps in and drapes his jacket over her shoulders."

Hope blinked in the song, but the overall feeling was still dark.

And then the music ended.

"Well?" Danny asked.

I shrugged. "Where's the rest of it?" I was getting into the story.

Reese's sigh was heavy. "There's no more. Did you hear it?"

I could be obtuse and ask *hear what*, but I did hear it. The entire melody was beautiful, but it was missing that spark that carried Reese's musical voice with it. "How does it sound on the keyboard?"

"The same, but more like *plink plink* than *pluck pluck*." Reese's reply was flat.

"I think it's closer than she's giving herself credit for," Danny said. "Right here, around the dancing"—he plucked out a few chords—"it falls off when it shouldn't."

Reese scowled. "But Cinderella realizes something is wrong, even though she's enjoying the night. She just hasn't put her finger on what it is yet."

Her almost-pout was cute. Kissable—

That was *not* where my mind needed to be. "How does the story end?"

Reese huffed. "Seriously? That's what you're hung up on?"

"Seriously. Spoil it for me." If this was Reese and Danny's rendition, it wasn't the same as the Disney movie. Not as dark as Grimm, but it would be different. "You're foreshadowing something the listener doesn't know yet, what is it?"

"Cinderella runs from the room. The prince's friend comes and finds her. He doesn't have to search because he knows exactly who she is. A child-hood friend he thought he'd never see again. Fuck the prince, she lives happily ever after with a man who actually knows her," Reese said.

I refused to draw any parallels between the story and her life, and sat in front of the keyboard instead. "Come here." I motioned for Reese to sit next to me. "Play the part Danny was talking about."

It sounded *very* different on piano than guitar, and it was both brighter and more haunting, but I still heard the bits that had them stalled.

"What about…" I went up an octave, and plucked out a few notes.

Reese scrunched her nose. "Mmm… Maybe this?" She responded with a variation on what I'd done.

"I like them both." Danny moved to stand next

to us, close enough my arm brushed his thigh when I hit the higher notes.

Reese and I went back and forth, countering and adding to each other's suggestions. As the tone of the music grew and surged, I felt the emotion tighten in my chest, but at the same time, it was like a floodgate was opened on my creativity. *Fuck* this felt good.

She moved forward in the song, and I knew where she was going with it. I added in a harmony, layered on top of what she had, and the sound in the room was incredible.

When we stopped, I was surprised. "Is there more?"

"Not yet. There will be." Reese grabbed a pencil and a blank score sheet and scribbled furiously.

Danny applauded. "That was fucking brilliant."

Reese's notes were sloppy and dashed on the page, but I didn't care. I could see where the music went. She stuck the sheet in front of us. "Help me out. Try this."

We started at the top, and the notes just *flowed*. I hit a few spots where she'd added something we hadn't tried yet, and my brain stumbled, but my fingers kept going. Those tweaks lifted the song even higher.

When we hit the end a second time, I was almost breathless. Why couldn't I do this at work? "Wow. You did it."

"We did it." Reese threw her arms around my neck and squeezed. "Brilliant. We're absolutely brilliant." She pulled back, but didn't take her arms away.

My pulse cranked to full volume and my thoughts stalled at the wild excitement that stared back at me. I'd be an idiot to ignore that something about collaborating with her—musically or sexually—was sparking my creativity.

But I'd be one-hundred percent moron to kiss her again.

Why wasn't Danny saying anything? Stopping us?

Reese licked her lips.

A tilt of my head, and I could do the same. Bite away that shine. See if her thrill matched the one throbbing inside me.

A flash threatened to disrupt the lock her gaze had on mine, but I didn't want to break this moment. I was half hard already. From whatever this was.

"Door." Danny's soft voice shattered the moment.

8 /
brandon

I forced myself to blink and scoot back, breaking the contact with Reese. "Someone should get that." I was already on my feet.

I scrubbed my face as I headed upstairs. I was vaguely aware of two pairs of footsteps behind me. When I opened the front door, I was surprised to see two uniformed police officers standing on the porch.

"Evening. We're looking for Adam Wilson," one said. "We understand he may be staying here?"

I glanced past them to the driveway. Adam's car wasn't here. "He is, but he's not here right now. Is something wrong?"

"We're investigating the fire on B Street. I believe he was staying there?"

I nodded. What the fuck did he do now?

"Standard investigation that the fire marshal does with any fire." The other officer handed me a card. "We just have a few questions for Mr. Wilson."

As in, arson? "I assure you, Adam wasn't involved." My brother was a lot of things, and I had to admit I could see him starting the fire accidentally, because he wasn't paying attention, but not arson. I took the card anyway.

Officer one shook his head. "No one is being charged with anything. Will you have him call us, and will you call us if you speak with Richard Hedd."

His business partner? "I'll do that." I closed the door, my mind racing. What the fuck did Adam get himself involved with this time?

I didn't want to think about it. It was too easy to summon the desire that was here moments earlier. I looked at Danny, not sure I trusted myself to look at Reese. I wanted them both, in different ways, but he wasn't off-limits. "Where were we? Composing, or…"

He raised an eyebrow, one corner of his mouth tugging up. "Pretty sure I was going to watch you kiss Reese, there was going to be another awkward moment where we all discussed whether or not it was okay, I was going to remind you I love a good show, and things were going to move forward from there."

"Excuse me." Reese's tone was sassy. "Do I get a say in this?"

I turned to her. "Always."

But she wasn't looking at me. "What if I'm the

one doing the kissing?"

"I still expect an incredible show." Danny grinned.

Reese stepped closer to me, a deceptively sweet smile in place, and molded her body to mine.

Was it dangerous to have this repeat performance? Reese and I were attracted to each other, but it wasn't as if we wanted the kind of emotional connection she and Danny had once upon a time. All of us agreed this was okay, we were adults, there was no problem.

I wanted to press her to the wall and fuck her here, but Adam could walk in. Why couldn't I completely fall into abandon? It didn't matter. I used my body to guide Reese backwards toward the bedroom.

The way she kissed me, the hunger with which I kissed back, was as frantic as that first night in Wendover. She shifted her body, vying to control the moment like she had before, but I wasn't having that tonight. When I gripped her neck and claimed her mouth, her laugh was tight with desire.

We quickly stripped each other down to nothing. She rubbed her naked body against mine, and the friction was need wrapped in anticipation.

I caught a glimpse of Danny as he made himself comfortable in the chair next to the bed, and stroked himself through his jeans. So. Fucking. Hot.

I pushed Reese onto the bed, and positioned her near the headboard. "Home court advantage."

"What does that mean?" She quirked her lips. "If you say it means you come first, I won't be impressed."

"It doesn't." And I was a little miffed she'd think that. I reached into the nightstand next to the bed and grabbed the handcuffs I kept within easy reach. I used my free hand to capture her wrists and pin them above her head, so I could cuff her to the headboard. "It means I know where the restraints are."

Reese squirmed, but didn't fight the restraints. Her writhing body was a stunning sight, and I didn't doubt she knew it. She had porcelain skin, the occasional pale freckle, and a dark landing strip between her legs that highlighted my target.

Danny dragged down his zipper and freed his cock to stroke it.

I took my time licking and sucking along Reese's neck and torso, loving the way her moans mingled with his as she twisted underneath me. I finally dragged my mouth down her stomach and buried my face between her legs.

She cried out when I licked along her already wet pussy, and she ground against my face. I devoured her juices and the delicious noises she made, diving my tongue inside her while I fingered her clit. When her ass rose off the bed, I pushed harder.

The noises Reese made when she came were their own kind of beautiful music, and I didn't let up until she was panting and jerking away.

Danny was next to me when I straightened, devouring Reese's taste on my lips, in a hungry, desperate kiss. His cock dug into my thigh.

I was so hard it hurt.

Danny stepped away. "Well, finish the show so I can finish too."

I didn't need to hear that twice. I rolled on a condom and knelt between Reese's legs. "Fuuuu-uck." Sliding inside her felt incredible. She wrapped her legs around my ass and pulled me in tighter, working her hips against me. I pounded to the pace she set, not wanting to hold back.

The familiar sounds of Danny's grunts as he came drilled into my thoughts. I picked up speed, letting control slip away as I slammed against Reese. I teased her clit as I hammered her, wanting her to get off again.

She clenched around me when she climaxed, milking me and stealing the last of my reason. I fucked with abandon, orgasm tightened in my balls and spilled from me. I was lost in the sensations— the sounds, the tastes, all of it.

The world slowly blurred back into view. I

uncuffed Reese, we cleaned up, and the three of us fell into bed together, me between her and Danny.

Inspiration sparked in my mind—a glow that wouldn't go away. A tune I wanted to get down before I lost it. As with the other night, this was a kind of creativity I'd been craving. I'd needed this feeling longer than I cared to admit.

Was the burst because of Reese? Why didn't this happen after sex with Danny?

It wasn't because I didn't love Danny. I did. More than anything. But with Reese, there was a taboo to it. The longer we did this, the more I ran the risk of her being with Danny as well, and there was still a hesitation that she might take him from me.

When I focused on the thought, I saw it wasn't true. If I were being rational, I knew Reese wasn't competition—not that way—she was a friend.

But the instinct was still there. Normal couples didn't do this—one didn't fuck the other's ex in front of him.

And I couldn't ignore the nagging that this would end poorly.

9 /
reese

I woke up to familiarity. A warmth and scent that summoned so many memories. Danny was wrapped around me. Why wasn't Brandon between us? And what would he think if he came back to this? I gently—reluctantly—extracted myself from Danny's arms, careful not to wake him.

The clock said it was a little after midnight. I didn't hear anyone in the bathroom, or any footsteps, though a faint light spilled in under the door. Where was Brandon?

He'd be back soon, I was sure. I couldn't stay here any longer tonight. If I woke up a second time like this with Danny…

It was easy enough to put the burden on Brandon and say he'd be upset, but I was selfish about this and more worried about me. It would get harder to pull away every time I found myself in Danny's arms.

I dressed as quietly as I could, and Danny slept through all of it. I crept from the room and toward the light in the kitchen. The light above the basement door was on—Brandon must be in there.

And Adam sat at the kitchen table, hunched over his laptop.

"Did I wake you?" he asked quietly.

I shook my head. "What are you doing?"

"Trying to figure out how to start over with zero capital." His frustration tugged at my sympathy.

"Do you mind company?" I should be leaving, but I couldn't make myself go.

He gestured to a chair, and I silently took a seat next to him.

"Is there anything I can do to help?" I asked.

He shook his head. "If I think of something, I'll let you know."

We sat in silence for a while as he typed.

"After my dad died, I looked for a long time to find someone who believed in me the way he did." Adam's quiet statement might as well have been a scream in the stillness.

"I know that feeling."

Adam sighed. "When I met Richard, and we clicked on a collaborative level, when he loved my ideas and was willing to invest, I thought *this is it*. I still want the plans I laid out with him."

Not quite the same as Plaid Peanut Butter, but close. "I know that feeling too."

"Yeah?" Adam looked at me with unguarded curiosity.

I tugged up a memory I usually tucked away just for me. I didn't know why, but with the quiet, contemplative mood in the room, it felt okay to talk about this. "Mom was my biggest fan. When she passed away, she made me promise I'd keep singing. Told me she'd be watching when I made it big." I was still waiting, and I hoped she was too.

"I didn't take her death well." The confession slipped out on its own. "I missed her so much, and I was so afraid of hurting that way again. Plus, I had this big promise to make good on. When Todd came along, offered me fame, and all I had to do was sever ties with the one other person who could hurt me if they left..." I couldn't finish the thought —my throat was too raw.

"I'm sorry," Adam said softly. "And I get it. My dad was sure I was going to be something amazing."

I couldn't ignore the surrender in his voice. "You will be." I was certain of it.

"I don't know that."

"I've got eight years on you, and I know I'm still going to break out. You've got plenty of time."

"Unless I end up like my dad. Brandon almost seems convinced of it."

I didn't understand why he phrased it that way. I knew their father had passed away, but I'd always assumed cancer or heart attack or… "What happened to your dad?"

"You don't know."

I shrugged apologetically. "Brandon and I aren't that kind of close."

"But you're fucking them, right?"

I didn't want to have this conversation with him. I wasn't even prepared to analyze my relationship with Danny and Brandon for myself. "We're just friends."

"Oh." Adam looked surprised. "The way you all are with each other, I figured it was just a matter of time before you moved in." He shook his head. "My dad. Suicide."

Holy fuck. "Goddess, I'm so sorry."

"I knew he was struggling, we both did, but we never thought…" Adam stared at his hands. "Even all these years later, I hear two voices. The one that asks if I could have stopped him and the one that asks if I'm next."

Was Brandon the same? Probably at least to some extent.

Adam shook his head hard, blinked a few times, and dragged in a shaky breath. "Wow. Sorry to dump on you."

"No. It's okay."

The basement door creaked, and Brandon stepped into the room. He looked between us. "Am I interrupting something?"

"Nope." The grief was gone from Adam's voice, replaced with false cheer.

"Okay." A soft smile played on Brandon's face, in sharp contrast to the conversation he'd walked in on. "The police were looking for you."

"I know. I talked to them," Adam said.

Brandon shifted from one foot to the other. "What did they want?"

"They asked me a bunch of questions about what I was doing when the fire started, if I was familiar with any insurance policies on the property, and if I knew where Richard was."

Brandon shifted his weight again. "I'm glad you're okay." He looked at me. "You coming back to bed?"

I wanted to, but that longing was still there to crawl back up to Danny's side. "I should get home."

"It's two in the morning."

Had I really been out here that long? And how much longer did that mean Brandon was in the music room? "Good reason for you to stop talking to us and go snuggle with your boyfriend."

Brandon nodded.

I grabbed my coat and trudged out to my car, letting the icy chill numb my heart. This was for the best.

10 /

reese

When I woke up, I was still thinking about last night.

I didn't click like I had with Brandon during collaboration with anyone except Danny. Brandon was a different flavor, though with him it was just as incredible to find that sweet spot where everything fit...

Like fucking each of them.

Nope. Wasn't going down that path. I was going to go about my Tuesday, work a little this morning, then pick up Adrienne early from work. A lot of the people at AcesPlayed had tattoos of the company's logo. She was planning to surprise her guys with hers, and wanted me to hold her hand.

I was good with that. Everyone needed a friend when they got their ink cherry popped.

My phone rang. Speaking of unsavory business relationships. I answered my manager's call. "Todd, hey. I was worried you didn't get my half dozen messages." I didn't try to hide my sarcasm.

"Yeah. I was busy. Holiday weekend and such."

So. Much. Bullshit. "The venue on Friday night was shit. Stinkier shit than normal. Are you going to deal with that?"

"No."

I grumbled a string of expletives under my breath. My contract was basic enough it didn't give me any loopholes, but it provided dozens of chances for him to take advantage of me. I might understand at least a little if he was booking me high paying gigs and keeping a large cut, but this wasn't doing anything for him either. It couldn't possibly be.

And now we'd have the same conversation we had every few months, and it wouldn't end any differently than it ever did. "Let me out of the contract, Todd. This arrangement isn't helping either of us." I kept my tone as cool and emotionless as possible, despite wanting to rage and call him a fucking idiot. Last few times I'd done that, the gigs got worse. "This isn't making you any more money than it is me."

"It's not about the money."

"What is it about?" Not that I expected him to tell me. He never had.

"I've gotta go. I'll email you your next gig when I have one."

Fucker. "What if I decide not to show up?"

"Then I'll sue you for breach of contract."

I screamed internally. This was like slamming my head into a brick wall over and over again. "Then just let me out of the fucking contract."

"No. Talk to you soon, Reese." He hung up.

I resisted the urge to throw my phone against the wall—I couldn't afford a new one—but I did scream at the top of my lungs. Fortunately, no one was home upstairs.

The contract was brutal in its simplicity. It said Todd owned all of my performances, in any format, live, tape, or otherwise, for the length of the contract.

The problem was, the contract didn't state a length or offer any terms for getting out of it. He'd offered to let me buy my way out a few times, always for a ridiculous amount of money.

Over the next couple of hours, both of my calls canceled on me. Instead of working, I spent hours searching for answers about my contract. I'd done this as well before, but every once in a while I stumbled on a new piece of information, or a new contact who was willing to give me a little bit of advice for free.

None of it had panned out yet, but I kept hoping.

Today wasn't going to be my day. By the time I left to pick up Adrienne from work, I was in the most ragey foul mood possible. Cranking the stereo and screaming along at the top of my lungs helped.

I got to the AcesPlayed building and texted Adrienne that I was here. Going inside to get her might ruin the surprise. It was easier to let myself think that, even though Dustin and Phillip would know she was leaving with me, than to admit I didn't want to see Brandon or Danny.

In this mood, I'd either transfer the frustration to Brandon, or hope one of them was up for an office quickie to release tension.

Such a bad idea.

Adrienne arrived before I could let my mind tug me toward *no, it's okay. Really. One more screw won't be a big deal*.

"Thank you so much for doing this with me." She hopped into the passenger seat. "I'm so nervous. Where on my body do you think I should get it?"

Thank the goddess for Adrienne. I never had to wonder what she was thinking, and I didn't have to worry about awkward silence. Between the two of us, we rarely stopped talking. "You haven't picked?"

"I mean… Yeah, but no?"

The way she made indecision sound so simple lightened my mood a hint. "Most everyone has them on their bicep." Obvious answer was obvious. But we had to start somewhere, and with any luck, finish before we reached the tattoo place.

"I know, but Sonya did hers on her shoulder blade, and it looks really cool, but a few of the guys said that hurt, but Chris said the arm one hurt too… And I want to be unique."

"You're getting the same artwork as almost the entire rest of the office," I said. "And they jam a needle in your skin over and over, to scar you. That's how it works. So… I don't know that you're on the right path for a unique, pain free experience."

Adrienne huffed. "I know. But a little less pain and a little more unique would be nice."

"What about on the outside of your calf or thigh? Don't think anyone else has one there, and it's a good place for kissing it better."

"Ooh, I didn't consider that. Bicep kisses aren't super sexy."

"I mean, it depends on who's doing the kissing. Maybe your guys aren't up to snuff."

Adrienne snorted. "Definitely not a problem. But also, I didn't shave my legs this morning. That's kind of weird."

"Not for those of us who are single. Are you getting lazy as a kept woman?" I teased.

"Maybe."

"They'll shave the area and I promise you they don't care, but if you're worried about it, bicep is probably your best bet."

Adrienne crossed her arms and sank lower in

her seat. "I don't know. Why can't I make up my mind? Maybe when I get there I'll flip a coin?"

I could tell her that was a bad idea, but I'd done worse. "Do you want me to pick for you?"

"No. But maybe. But yes. Okay."

"Then do your bicep." I didn't care if she rejected the idea. I expected she would since she'd had so much resistance to it up to this point.

She puffed out a long breath. "Okay. Outside of my calf it is."

She was just the right level of indecisive. Decisive? Either way, I loved it.

We got to the tattoo parlor, and I introduced her to the woman who'd done most of my ink.

Adrienne rolled up the leg of her jeans. "Sorry about the fuzz."

"I promise you, I've seen worse." Etta snapped on a pair of gloves. "Let's get started." She walked through setting everything up while she explained to Adrienne how the process would work. When she leaned in and turned on the needle, Adrienne gripped my hand tightly.

"Ouch." Adrienne whimpered.

Etta laughed. "I haven't started. Low pain threshold?"

"We're about to find out," Adrienne said.

Etta touched the needle to Adrienne's leg, and earned a wince in return, but Adrienne sat without squirming or complaining through the entire thing.

When the work was done, Adrienne admired it both from above and in the mirror, and grinned. "I love it. The guys at work are wimps."

"As is frequently the case." While Etta cleaned up and wrapped the tattoo in plastic, she ran Adrienne through caring for the ink while it healed.

Adrienne was tentative when she put more weight on her leg, and then she was fine. We headed back to my Jeep. "Dresses next," she said.

I tried to hide my wince, but it slipped out anyway. I didn't have money for a new evening gown, but I could hit the discount racks and make something work. Mom had taught me a lot about building a gorgeous outfit from thrift store chic, I just didn't expect to still be needing the knowledge all these years later.

"Sure. Dresses next." It was why she told Phillip and Dustin we were taking this trip; she needed to come back with something.

Dustin had planned their company Christmas party this year, and for some reason decided it should be a formal affair. Since I hadn't seen this group do anything like this in the past, I assumed Adrienne, and possibly Luna, had some influence on that decision.

When I happily agreed to be Adrienne's date, I hadn't realized *fancy dress* was on the play list.

Adrienne squeezed my hand, though not as hard as she had in the tattoo parlor. "I get it. It hasn't been that long since I was strapped for cash. You can drop me off if you'd rather, but I'd love your opinion."

Damn it. I wanted to go dress shopping, even if I couldn't afford it. "Let's go. Point me in a direction."

She gave me directions to a little boutique tucked away from downtown traffic. When we stepped inside, my bank account whimpered and I had *Pretty Woman* flashbacks. Not the scene where Richard Gere gave Julia Roberts the necklace, but the one where she tried to go shopping on Rodeo Drive and the salespeople snobbed her out of the store.

I wouldn't be finding any clearance racks in here. But I did help Adrienne pick out a few styles and colors.

Adrienne tried on several dresses, but the one that looked best on her had a strap on one shoulder and left the other bare. The bodice hugged her torso, in a gradient of white to gold, and flowed into a black skirt that just brushed the ground when she was in heels.

"You look amazing," I said.

She pointed to a strapless satin dress in a rich purple that looked like it would hug the body all the way down, with a slit up one leg to make walking possible. "You need to try on that one. Excuse me."

She gestured to the sales lady. "Can we get this in her size?"

A few minutes later, Adrienne was zipping me into the dress. It fit perfectly and made me look *good*. The price tag scared me though. It was more than I spent on clothes in an entire year. Enough to buy me a guitar. Not a high-end one, but middle of the road.

"You look amazing." Adrienne's voice was all awe.

I twisted this way and that in front of the three-way mirror. I really did look incredible.

"We'll take them both," Adrienne told the saleswoman.

I grabbed Adrienne's arm. "No we won't." I tried to keep my voice quiet. She'd found the one thing that embarrassed me.

"Give us a minute." Adrienne smiled at the clerk, then grabbed my hand and tugged me to a quiet corner of the store. "Please," she said. "Let me buy this for you."

My humiliation climbed higher. "Please don't ask."

Adrienne looked me in the eye. "I told you, I know how it feels. You *know* I do." The entire time, she spoke quietly enough only I would hear her, but it had to be obvious what we were talking about. "I got a good bonus, we're splitting our expenses three ways at home, and I want to do this for you. It doesn't put me out. It doesn't change my opinion of you. You look *amazing* in that dress."

If I were talking to anyone else, I'd question their sincerity, but it was impossible to do that with Adrienne. In her place, I'd want to do the same thing for friends. I'd probably buy non-stop presents for months for Danny and everyone if I had extra spending money. And I did love the dress. "Okay. But I'm paying you back as soon as I can." I was already doing the math in my head to figure out how much I could give her a month.

"You really don't have to, but yay." She gave me a big hug, and turned back to the clerk. "I'll take them both."

I hated this so much. Always relying on other people and being so incapable of providing for myself.

11 /
danny

When Brandon crawled into bed, the night he and Reese fucked at home, he'd woken me up.

"Where's Reese?" I asked. "Where were you?" The pair of questions pushed aside my sleepiness.

"She had to go. I was working. Composing."

The first answer hurt, and the second one surprised me, but I was happy he'd found inspiration a second time. It was better to focus on the latter. "How'd it go?"

Brandon wrapped himself around me. "Beautifully. Get some more sleep."

I hadn't. It took hours for me to doze off again after he passed out.

And several days later, I was still rolling the brief exchange over and over in my mind. I'd brought it up a few times since, and Brandon didn't think it was a big deal.

I spent the rest of the week between contract work at AcesPlayed, and working with groups at the shelter, and by Friday night, I was ready for the fun that came next.

Brandon and I followed the signs in the downtown hotel that directed us to the AcesPlayed Holiday Party. When we reached the ballroom, I had to pause in the doorway and take it all in.

Dustin had outdone himself this time. The room had been transformed from basic and bland. Evergreen branches, lights, and tasteful ribbons decorated the walls, and the two long tables lining the room had the perfect rustic feel to them.

It was my understanding he got a bigger budget than normal, because this wasn't just a holiday party, it was a celebration of their game being in beta, and that they'd made it this far.

The entire affair included an open bar, and discounted hotel rooms for anyone who didn't want to drive home after taking advantage of it. Brandon and I wouldn't be drinking, but we did have a room, so we could step away from the world at the end of the night.

I loved all of it. The look, the setting, and the suits. Brandon looked sexy as fuck.

We weren't the first to arrive, but we were close. We tracked down Dustin long enough to tell him everything looked great, then let him get back to running the show. Nigel and Jeremy were here, too.

Somehow Nigel managed to get on Luna's bad side her first few weeks with the company—I didn't think she had such a thing, but apparently so—I thought he was a nice guy, though.

Actually, I liked most of the people at Aces-Played. This last week in the office had been a lot of fun. The work, the colleagues... I wouldn't go back to cybersecurity full time, but it was nice to dig in and get my hands dirty every once in a while.

We chatted with Phillip between his helping Dustin, and flitted from group to group as more people wandered in.

A sharp wolf whistle that had to be Dustin's echoed through the room, and I turned toward the door. He was whistling for Adrienne, but I couldn't tear my gaze from Reese. The way that dress hugged her, the slit up the side to almost her thigh, and the way she held herself like royalty.

"*Fuck me*," Brandon's murmur matched my thoughts.

Did he know he'd said that aloud? Regardless, I liked it.

Most everyone else went back to their conversations, but my eyes were glued on Queen Reese as she and her date strode toward us.

"I'm going to go say *hi* to Dustin, be right back," Adrienne gave us a short wave and wandered away.

I twirled my finger. "Give us a spin," I said to Reese.

Pink splashed across her cheeks, unusual for her but stunning, and she twirled in the dress. "I feel like a grown-up." Her tone said *joking*, but a hint of seriousness lay underneath.

"You look beautiful." I kissed her on the cheek. As I pulled away, *more* whispered through my mind.

Brandon grasped her fingers and kissed the back of her knuckles. "You look more than beautiful. We could get Jeremy over here to come up with a better word for it."

"I think I get your point." Reese's easy smile was back, erasing any embarrassment. "You both look pretty fucking hot too."

Brandon raised an eyebrow. "Of course we do."

The conversation lulled. Why was there any pause at all? I couldn't be the only one of us thinking about the sparks the two of them had been generating.

I could ignore that ache to be with her again when she wasn't around, but looking at her now, next to Brandon, seeing the two of them strip out of their evening wear was all I could think about.

It was a dangerous path to let my desire wander down, but that didn't mean I could stop myself.

When Luna arrived with Graham and Cole, it was a good excuse to break up the lack of conversation and say *hi*. Cole knew almost everyone in the room, and not because he'd been working with Luna and I for the last few days to update computers. He'd been one of the original employees at Rinslet, and he'd retired from the gaming industry early.

He was also Judith's ex-husband, but their divorce was older than Brandon's and my relationship. The two of them were friends-ish these days.

Wow. Reese was right, we really were grown-ups. I looked around the room, able to put a name to every face, and a pleasant memory to almost as many people. How many of them realized what an incredible family this was?

A little past the top of the hour, Dustin asked everyone to have a seat, because dinner would start soon, and he promised other fun after.

I wasn't surprised at the way everyone broke up to claim the two tables. Creative teams were next to each other, Dev was by itself—though to be fair they were half the company. Judith sat at one table and Cole was at the opposite end of the room at the other.

But his choice had nothing to do with her. Luna was sitting near us, and Cole would move mountains for her. So would Graham. Taking a seat next to her was a no brainer.

I'd love to have something similar with Brandon and Reese. Yes, I was seated by them, but the moving mountains thing... Thinking the words made them feel more real, but I wouldn't sacrifice what I had with Brandon to try to get there.

Chatter faded to the occasional snippet of conversation while everyone ate. I couldn't keep my gaze from drifting to Reese, who sat across from us with Adrienne and Luna. Reese always looked like royalty, but tonight...

And she belonged here, with all of us. She and Adrienne had become quick friends over the last few months. This little pocket of people, with the decorations and Christmas music, it all warmed me from the inside out.

As dinner wound down, and the catering crew carted away plates, Nigel shouted, "What's the stage for?" The slight slur in his words was indicative of the drinks he'd had. "Awards ceremony? Speeches?"

"It's not ours," Dustin said. "It was here when we got here, and we couldn't find anyone to take it away, so we decorated it with the rest of the room and made sure there were lots of lights on it."

"Aww." Luna sounded disappointed.

Elliot rose halfway in his seat, enough to see her. "There's no way you're upset about extra lights."

"I'm not." Luna huffed. "But I was hoping the stage meant something."

"We could play charades."

I couldn't see who made the suggestion.

Judith shook her head. "Definitely not with this group when half of you are drunk. Clothes will come off."

"What's wrong with that?" Chris—one of the developers—asked.

Reese smirked. "First time I think I've ever agreed with that asshole," she muttered.

"How about a talent show," Nigel suggested.

"Being anal retentive isn't a talent." Chris apparently had opinions tonight. "You were born that way."

Elliot raised a few fingers. "Hang on. I want to know what Nigel's actual talent is."

Nigel pushed back from the table, and a hush fell over the room. When he grabbed the steak knife next to his plate, and then Jeremy's and Judith's knives, several people gasped.

"Whoa. Hang on." Judith reached for him.

Jeremy stopped her. "Trust him."

Nigel stepped away from the table to a clearing near the front of the room, and hefted the knives a few times. Then he started to juggle.

"Holy shit. Did you know he could do that?" I asked Brandon.

Brandon shook his head, his attention never leaving Nigel.

Nigel stopped, spun, and tossed the knives one at a time at the stage. All three stuck in the middle of a wreath hanging on the front of the structure.

The room erupted in applause.

Dustin joined Nigel at the front of the room. "Talent show is over. Unless someone can beat that without causing an insurance incident." Dustin finished his announcement with more applause and pointed Nigel toward his seat.

Laughter rippled around us.

"Reese and Danny can." Adrienne spoke above the chatter. "Maybe not beat it, but they can compete."

Reese stared at her.

Adrienne shrugged. "What? It's true."

"They don't work here, they don't count." Nigel sounded put out.

"I assure you, they do." Brandon's voice was hard.

I didn't want this to escalate. The night had been nice so far. "I guarantee we can't compete with knife juggling."

"But will you sing anyway?" Luna asked. "Nigel only used part of the stage. The rest still needs love."

It did sound like fun, and Reese had to be itching to cave. I was surprised when she said, "There are no instruments."

Like that had ever mattered to us before.

"Sing. Sing. Sing. Sing." Luna started the chant and half the room joined in. An unusual display of enthusiasm from the Dev side of the room.

I exchanged looks with Reese, and she was chewing her bottom lip. I stood and offered my hand, and she accepted as I pulled her to her feet.

We drew almost as much applause as Nigel and we hadn't done anything yet.

"Do you want music?" Brandon asked softly.

Reese shook her head. "We'll keep things low key."

That hardly seemed like us, but okay. As we walked to the stage together, we quickly discussed what we were going to perform. It didn't take much to decide—we had a medley of Christmas songs we performed whenever it was appropriate, and it was always a hit.

The mics on stage didn't work, but it didn't matter. This crowd, this setup, was perfection compared to some of our recent gigs. I stepped to the front of the stage. "First of all, another round of applause for Nigel, because *holy shit* dude."

Everyone in the room clapped again, and as it died down, I looked at Reese. She moved her lips as she counted, but no sound came out, and she slid into the opening strains of *Silent Night*.

12 /
brandon

I was as in awe as everyone around me as Reese dove into a soulful rendition of *Silent Night*, with Danny offering a baritone harmony. Their voices blended beautifully, the way they always did, as the pair slid through three or four more songs. The tempo kicked up when Reese started in on *All I Want for Christmas is You*. Mariah Carrey had nothing on her.

It was impossible to ignore the flashes of chemistry between Danny and Reese as they sang to each other. Tonight I swore I could taste it though. How were they still apart, after all this time? And how amazing would it be to become a part of their dynamic? I wasn't jealous—I didn't want to break them apart—I wanted that cohesiveness the three of us had the other night in the basement.

They looked amazing up there. Danny in his

suit, Reese in her dress. If I didn't know Danny was mine, I'd assume they were the perfect couple.

As they finished, more clapping filled the air. Danny and Reese descended, joining the rest of us. Most everyone stepped up to tell them how great they sounded. Reese ate up the praise. Danny shrugged a lot of it off.

When I was able to get close enough, I pulled Danny away from the adoring audience, and let them focus on Reese.

"Should we ask her if she wants to stay?" My question came out before I could consider the consequences.

Danny studied my face, as if looking for the right reply. "I don't know how to answer that."

"It's not a trick question. There's no wrong answer." Though I was hoping he'd say *yes*.

His frown was surprising. "I don't know how well I'll handle another round of the two of you together, keeping my hands to myself. I don't mind most of the time, but tonight…"

The air was different. Charged. There was one concession I wasn't ready to make, though. "I can't watch her with you."

"I don't need that. As long as I don't have to keep my hands off you," Danny said.

"Is that a *yes*?"

Danny nodded. "From me it is. You still have to negotiate with Reese."

That sounded like a good plan to me. Everyone was splitting off into the same pockets they did in the office, some talking about going home or to their rooms and others chatting some more.

Reese was talking to Adrienne and Phillip, and I joined them. "May I steal your date for the night?" I asked Adrienne.

She looked at Reese. "I don't think that's up to me."

"I have candy in my van, little girl," I said teasingly to Reese.

She smirked. "Not in your pocket?"

"Only one way to find out."

Reese's smile grew. "We'll catch you two later. Tell Dustin it was a great party."

When she and I reached Danny again, Reese slipped her hands in my front pockets. She teased my cock through the thin fabric. "I don't think that's candy," Reese said.

Danny raised his brows. "Is this where someone inserts a joke about sucking on it to find out?"

"Insert. Penis. I see what you did there." Reese pressed her touch harder into me.

I drew her hands out. "Does that mean I can convince you to come back to our room with us?"

Reese looked at me, eyes wide and expression deceptively innocent. "What about the van?"

"We don't have a van. Why would you think

there was a van?" Danny's confusion was as fake as Reese's naiveté.

I shook my head. "I think the candy analogy has run its course."

"Thank fuck, because I'd rather have some good dick than a piece of candy," Reese said.

Danny snorted a laugh, and the three of us headed toward the elevator. We stepped into the lift with two other couples.

Reese stood next to me. "But seriously, what's the plan?"

Danny was on my other side. "We were waiting for you, to discuss specific details."

"It's assumed that tabs and slots are involved." I kept my reply intentionally vague.

It didn't seem to matter, since one person huffed and another laughed.

Reese cast a glance in their direction. "That's too bad. I was looking for dicks. Pretty sure I already said that."

It was probably a good thing both couples got off at the next floor. I pressed into Reese's back and glided a hand up her bare leg, thanks to the slit in her dress. "Would you rather watch or be watched?"

"What do you think?" Reese countered. "Are we giving the guy on the other side of the security camera a show?"

That was tempting—stop the elevator and finger her right here until she came. Here. The idea sent a rush through me. I had grasp of the sensibility to keep from doing so, but I hooked her dress over her hip, glided my hands along the edge of her panties and teased between her legs.

Her gasp was as delicious as Danny's soft moan.

"She could do both, couldn't she?" Danny asked.

Reese leaned more of her weight against me, and her heat seared through my skin. "Watching and being watched?"

"That sounds delicious," I growled against her neck.

We reached our floor, and the three of us walked to the room. The suite inside was stunning and spacious with a balcony overlooking the city. If it was warmer, it would be tempting to fuck out there. I unzipped Reese's dress without hesitation.

She stepped out of the dress, leaving her in panties, stockings, and shoes. She held herself with the same grace and poise as if she were walking across the stage fully clothed, and *fuck* she was gorgeous. There was a couch near the balcony and a chair with an ottoman across from that. She perched on the chair, back straight and legs crossed at the knee.

I knew I wasn't the only one watching her, captivated, as she uncrossed her legs, ala Sharon Stone, but in Reese's case, there was no pausing for a frame or two for a glimpse of what she was showing off.

She set both feet on the floor, legs together, gaze on us.

This was at least as scorching as feeling her up in the elevator.

Palms on her knees, she parted her legs. She drew her fingers up the inside of her thighs, and paused three-quarters of the way up. A single strip of red satin and lace covered her pussy. "I was promised this show went both ways." Reese's voice was husky.

She didn't have to say that again. I turned to Danny and worked his tie loose to let it hang around his neck. While I trailed my fingers down the front of his shirt, undoing every button I encountered, he cupped me through my slacks, teasing my cock and drawing it from half to completely hard.

We took our time undressing each other, stripping away clothes in between stealing kisses, running our hands over each other, and stroking erections. The moans and groans that filled the room were the perfect intro to the song we were creating.

When Danny and I were naked, we settled on the couch, attention half on each other and half on Reese.

A soft smile played on her face as she cupped her breasts and played with her nipples. Her lips were slightly parted, and pink flushed her skin.

Danny stroked me, and I stroked him, keeping a perfect rhythm.

Reese slid her panties down her legs and kicked the red G-string aside, exposing herself. Incredible sight, especially with her as fascinated by us as I was by her.

She teased herself, gliding fingers over slick skin, then dipping in her opening. She pumped slowly, her moans growing louder in a slow build.

I was intoxicated by Danny's touch, by his hot shaft in my hand, and by the flush running over Reese's body. Her gasps. Danny's grunts. The orchestra of the sounds we made was as good as any collection of instruments.

Reese's chest heaved in a more erratic pattern, and she moved her fingers to her clit. Her eyelids fluttered. She licked her lips. Sighs became moans became cries as she sped toward crescendo. No, not crescendo—changeover.

She tensed as she came, orgasm shuddering through her body, then sank back into the chair.

The show was as good seeing her basking in bliss as watching her finger herself, though neither Danny nor I were stroking as fast.

When she pressed her fingers to her lips and sucked them clean, my need spiked.

The solo was over, but it flowed perfectly into the next verse.

Reese crossed the room, and I pulled her toward

me before it was clear which direction she was heading. Danny's touch fell away when she draped her arms around my neck, and I returned my fist to my own cock.

"It was lonely over there." The pout in Reese's tone was a silky touch over my skin.

"We're happy to have you closer," I said.

She straddled one of my legs, grinding her wet pussy against my bare thigh.

Fuck, this was a better part two than I would've composed. The sounds Danny made were a harmony of agreement.

Reese leaned forward and pressed a breast to my mouth.

I parted my lips in acceptance, drawing a nipple into my mouth to lick and suck.

She worked her hips harder and I did the same with my fist around my shaft. Fingers brushed my legs—Danny's—but I was too caught up in the intensity of this to mind. Reese's expression was classic beauty when she climaxed a second time, and she worked herself against my leg until she was spent.

Danny pressed his fingers to her lips, and I watched with fascination and desire as she sucked herself from his skin.

I lost myself in the orgasm building inside. Tightening in my balls. Pulsing under my skin. Hammering in my ears. I wasn't sure if Danny or I finished first. I was too absorbed in the music and the light show exploding behind my eyelids.

Sticky white coated my hand and stomach. My leg was just as much a mess thanks to Reese, and I assumed Danny was the same. Contentment filled my thoughts. This was the kind of incredible some people searched a lifetime for.

I woke up to Reese letting out a long string of curses. "What's wrong?" My question was groggy as I pushed into a sitting position.

She pointed the screen of her phone at me.

It was too early to do this without glasses. I fumbled for mine on the nightstand, but I heard the music before I put them on. It was a recording of her and Danny from last night.

"Is that YouTube?" Danny asked sleepily.

"Worse. It's TwangView. One of your lovely colleagues posted us online, and the video has hundreds of thousands of views."

I never thought I'd hear Reese so upset about going viral, but she sounded pissed.

13 /
reese

I should be celebrating. Popping the cork on a bottle of champagne. We had a video go viral. *Us*. Fuck the detractors, almost everyone loved it.

And instead I was eating the TUMS in my purse like candy, as I played back the early morning voice mail for Brandon and Danny that I'd gotten from my manager.

"I knew you'd fuck up eventually." Todd's voice was even more grating when it was on speaker phone. "I'm surprised it took this long, but the moment the courts open in the morning, your ass is mine." I hung up the phone.

"I mean, technically even if he manages to serve you tomorrow, it'll be at least a few weeks before your ass is his." Danny's voice was forced-light.

Brandon climbed out of bed. "Maybe he can get the courts to pull the stick out of his ass while he's there."

"You're not helping." I was so stressed out I didn't even watch Brandon cross the room to his bag. I wasn't enjoying that we were in a hotel nice enough to have bathrobes.

I wanted desperately to be loving this moment. I'd dreamed of something like our music going viral and us drawing in a huge new fanbase. Possibly even masturbated to the fantasy. But not like this.

Danny crawled toward the foot of the bed where I was sitting. Waking up with them, not one bed over, but sharing the same space, had been a wonderful kind of warm fuzzy. Until I'd checked my voicemail.

"What do we need to do?" Danny asked.

"Clothes. Please." Yeah, I was watching my career implode and I cared that his dick was hanging out.

Or maybe I was being melodramatic. Maybe this was the turning point I'd been waiting for. Todd would finally figure out this partnership wasn't beneficial to either of us, and I could move on with my life.

"Mine or yours?" Danny asked. He snagged the pair of boxer briefs Brandon tossed him, and stood to put them on. The lightweight dark fabric didn't hide much more than him staying naked, but it was something.

"I don't know what to do." Being jarred into this

state of panic so early in the morning had my brain on the fritz. I needed coffee. Or vodka. Or to wake up and realize this was all just a nightmare.

Danny reached for my phone. "Who posted the video?"

I unlocked it, brought up the right page, and handed it over. "I don't know. No profile pic. RenobXOX?"

"Boner kisses?" Danny raised his brows. "Does sound like one of us." He looked at the screen, then showed it to Brandon.

Brandon scrolled through the screen. "Don't know the name. If they're with Aces, they're not going to tell anyone this is theirs. About half this account violates our code of conduct."

A lot of people thought it was counterintuitive for a company that made a game featuring graphic sex to have rules about what their employees could and couldn't say in public. But as a group, Aces was hyper aware of not doing things that would draw them more negative attention. They had some of the strictest no harassment rules out there.

None of which helped me right now.

Brandon pressed his phone to his ear. The muffled strains of someone answering the other end filtered out, but not loud enough to make out words. "Hey. You guys still here?"

The response sounded like an adult from a

Charlie Brown cartoon. The absurdity of the thought almost made me cackle.

"What are the odds you brought your laptop?" Brandon asked.

More muffled words.

Maybe it was like Kenny on South Park.

Brandon almost cracked a smile. "Fucking work-a-holic, I knew it. I need a favor. DCMA… Now would be good… I'll send you the link, and I owe you." He disconnected and set his phone on the nightstand. "Dustin is getting the video taken down. He's got a dozen processes in place, just like with the crowdfunded game," Brandon said.

A glimmer of relief seeded in my chest. It couldn't be this easy, but I felt like I could breathe again. "What next?"

Brandon gave Danny a questioning look.

Danny frowned and shook his head.

"Why not?" Brandon asked.

Danny stared back at him in disbelief. "What do you mean *why not*? I have no idea what you're asking me."

That almost made me laugh. "Do you want me to cover my ears? Leave the room? Go hide in the bathroom so you can talk?"

"No." Brandon's huff was amused. "What I was asking him"—he gave Danny a pointed look—"was since we have the room through tomorrow, if we should grab our laptops, get you something more comfortable to wear than the dress, and have a mini-vacation LAN party."

"Gosh, why the fuck didn't I guess that from your sternly furrowed brow?" Danny's retort was playfully sarcastic. "When have we ever done that?"

This time I did laugh. "Careful Brandon, your roots are showing."

He patted the top of his head. "I'm not going gray yet. This is all natural."

"Mostly," Danny said.

My smile grew bigger. "I meant your gaming roots. Who does that? Who gets a hotel room and spends the weekend playing games?"

"I guarantee you almost everyone I work with has done it at least once." Brandon's retort carried a hint of *duh*.

"My point exactly," I said.

"Do you have work today?" Brandon asked.

I shook my head.

"So, you're going to go home and spend the weekend cycling over this problem, not knowing how bad it is, not able to do anything, until Monday morning." Danny summed the situation up nicely.

I shrugged in acceptance.

"You owe me a game, it's a good way to be distracted, problem solved."

It was tempting to argue with Brandon's logic, if for no other reason than I didn't like him assuming I'd say *yes*, but I really didn't like the idea of being stuck alone with my own thoughts for the next two days.

Besides, I'd heard a *lot* about this game, and it was time to see how much of the worship from its creators was true. And if my staying here led to another night like last night, even better. "Let me go grab my laptop, and change, and I'm in."

I wasn't doing a walk of shame wearing this dress home—stupid phrase. There was no shame in what we'd done and it was a gorgeous dress. Who knew when I'd have the excuse to wear it again? Fuck it, I'd make a reason for this dress. I hung it on a hook on the wall, so I could see it from anywhere in my apartment, prepared for a day and a night of fun—whatever that may entail—and headed back to the hotel.

As I was pulling into the parking lot, my phone chimed with a new text, and then another. By the time I parked, my phone had stopped chirping.

I scrolled through the string of messages from Dustin.

It's down.

I assume it was yours.

I think it was hotel staff.

I'll talk to them.

The decision to sing was mine, and anyone who recorded it didn't know doing so might cause me issues. I sent him back a quick, *Don't get anyone in trouble. And thank you.*

Maybe it would be okay. There was a free legal service I'd talked to about this contract in the past, and if Todd really did try to sue me, they could help me figure it out. Or this would be the moment he realized managing me wasn't doing anyone any favors.

Hell, even if he saw the popularity of the video and it started getting me better gigs, I'd take that.

It'd be fine. I'd be fine.

Please let this be fine.

I caught up to Danny in the lobby, near the elevators. He had two laptop bags slung over his shoulder.

"You lost the *go fetch stuff* coin toss?" I teased.

"Brandon wanted to get something down. You know how inspiration goes."

There was something off about Danny's reply. Not unhappiness but a tone I couldn't place. I studied his face in the reflection of the door as we rode the elevator up, but all I saw was a warped version of his natural smile bouncing back at me.

When we reached the room, we set up our laptops so we could play. Danny had a portable hotspot we logged into, insisting Luna would have someone's hide if we used hotel wi-fi. Not that we'd be able to play with that kind of connection.

Brandon was surprised I already had the game installed.

"Adrienne hooked me up." I owed her a game later. "But you get to be my first time."

Danny smirked and Brandon raised an eyebrow. But the instant I was on the character creation screen, Brandon was there pointing things out and walking me through steps.

I picked a character race that was tall and slender, with pale skin and pointy ears, and I loved that she was wearing basically a black version of the strappy outfit from *The Fifth Element*. She had two swords, and did a nifty spin-kick-slash animation every time I moused over her.

When I got in the game, Brandon and Danny's characters were waiting outside the beginning area.

"First quest is this way." Brandon's eager tone matched the way his avatar bounced around me.

The quest was *Hunt Five Droidlings* if the text on the right side of my screen was accurate. "I mean…" I didn't want to kill Brandon's excitement, but "Do I have to do the beginner quests *now*? I was promised orgies and nudity. Hunting droidlings isn't the kind of sword play I signed up for."

Danny and Brandon looked at me like I was speaking a foreign language.

"I thought you wanted to play the game," Brandon said.

"I do." I hadn't gone into this completely clueless—I wasn't a gamer, but I understood the basics. "But right now I want to *experience* it."

Danny nudged Brandon. "There's that strip club that Sonya and Phillip are really proud of."

I stared at Danny with disbelief. "A *strip club*? Seriously?"

"No, he's right. If you want to experience the game, that's as good a starting point as any." Brandon grinned. "You don't have to believe me, but trust Danny on this."

It took me a minute or two of fiddling with my keyboard to get the hang of walking. I followed them through some stunning and vibrant scenery, to a part of the game town that was lit with a lot of neon. I had to admit, that looked pretty neat.

I wasn't sure what to make of the silhouette on the sign outside the club we walked up to, but when we stepped through the door and the new setting loaded, it all made sense. It was a male strip club, with some scantily clad orcs both on stage and serving drinks.

"Wow." I wasn't sure if it was a good exclamation or a bad one. This was certainly fascinating. I wasn't going to yuck anyone's yum, but this wasn't doing anything sexual for me. "It's warped and weird and fantastic. What else do you have like this?"

"This way, my dear." Danny's avatar made a sweeping bow motion as he spoke.

As they led me through the town—a vast maze that would take me days to get comfortable with on my own—they pointed out different spots. Training halls, brothels, clothing, upgrade shops, and more. I saw Phillip's and Dustin's influence in the art, and even in a few places where hints of Adrienne's influence showed through, though she hadn't been with the company long enough for a lot of her art to be released.

I recognized Sonya's nearly fourth wall breaking sense of humor in some of the NPC's, based on the few conversations I'd had with her.

And overlapping all of it, Brandon's scores brought it all together. His music was seamless and stayed in the background unless one was looking for it. I was, and the sound was incredible.

There was one thing missing from my experience still. "Where's this explicit sex I keep hearing about?"

"Brothel, hotel, any club that advertises public sex. Do you have a preference?" Brandon asked.

I shrugged. "Whatever lets me see what the hype is about."

We got a room at a nearby hotel. As my character went to walk through a door, a series of on-screen confirmations popped up. The warnings were directly blunt that I was about to see nudity and sexual content. I should leave if I didn't want to experience it, and I could walk away at any time I was uncomfortable.

I accepted all of it, and my screen loaded a

cyberpunk looking hotel room with mirrored ceilings, a round bed in the middle, and borderline seventies porn music. A glance away from my screen showed Brandon watching me with expectation.

"Is the room for the gamer, or for you and Dustin to show off your mad skills?" I asked.

He raised his brows. "It can be both."

I didn't have an argument. "So how does this work?"

They walked me through the different emotes, and how the matching on screen actions changed, depending on if one, two, or all three of us were involved. "It's cartoon people having sex." I tilted my head as Danny's avatar took Brandon's cock in his mouth, and Brandon's character fingered mine. It was definitely pornographic, and the art was stunning and anatomically correct. "It's certainly beautiful work, but…"

"It's a different kind of role playing," Brandon said.

"I get the appeal, I do. But it's not doing it for me." I felt a little bad saying so. Like I was missing a bigger picture.

Danny stood and moved to stand behind me. What in the…?

"It's not?" he asked.

I shook my head.

His hot breath caressed my neck when he

moved his mouth near my ear. He wasn't making contact, but his heat teased my senses.

I was intently aware of Brandon watching us, and that the amusement was fading from his eyes, leaving a mask in its place.

"Not even if you're with the right person?" Danny's tone was low, and as seductive as his nearness. "Their voice in your ear as they murmur all the things they'd like to do to you?"

It was too tempting to close my eyes and sink into him. A lean back and he'd support my weight. A shift to the left and his lips would brush my ear.

"Like take me carburetor shopping?" I forced myself to joke.

"Like drop to their knees and worship at your feet," Danny said. "Like bury their face between your legs and lick your pussy until you're panting and writing in pleasure, and then they keep going."

This was what I fought so hard to forget about Danny. He was summoning the memories I fought to ignore when I was with Brandon. Even now, with Brandon watching us, his expression unreadable, I couldn't push my desire aside. I couldn't ignore how much I loved Danny's voice in my ear. Loved the way he made my pulse race. Loved tasting him.

How much I loved hi—

I pulled away. "You know what? I was mistaken earlier." I shut my laptop with a *thumk*. "I do have work today. I'm sorry. I can't believe I forgot." I was on my feet, fumbling to get everything shoved in its bag. "I've gotta go. Brandon, you owe me a mall trip. Bye." I stumbled out the door.

My lie was obvious and I didn't care. I needed to leave now, before I gave into the temptation to be with Danny again.

14 /
brandon

I struggled to process my emotions about what I'd just seen. Danny behind Reese, millimeters from kissing her, and her looking very much like she wanted nothing more. I knew this was coming between the two of them, and had been fighting the reality.

Reese's lie was obvious, and if my mind was working, maybe I'd stop her from leaving. But if she stayed...

I didn't know what came next because my mind refused to process.

And then she was gone.

I turned to Danny. "What was that?"

"I got caught up in the moment. That's all." Danny's lie was as obvious as Reese's, and hurt more.

"What are we doing?" I was asking myself as much as I was him.

He sank into a nearby chair. Only a few feet away, but it felt like so much more. "What kind of an answer do you want? Something emotionless and analytical? Something that makes light of the situation?"

I raked my fingers through my hair. "I want the answer that tells me what the right next step is. Or at least one that lets me throw caution to the wind long enough to not care."

"There are far worse times to do that than with Reese." Was that a hint of hopefulness in Danny's voice? Could I lie to myself any longer that it would be anything but?

Maybe if I voiced my thoughts, I'd have an easier time remembering why they mattered. "She's your ex-girlfriend."

"She's our current friend."

"She almost destroyed you."

Danny winced. "She tried to destroy herself and I got caught in the crossfire."

"That doesn't change what she did to you." That was easy for me to remember. How much their splitting up hurt Danny. How lost he was when we met.

He frowned. "You're the one fucking her."

"But you want to be." I knew this was coming, since that first night I was with Reese. Longer. Since the first time, years ago, when Danny let his defenses down around her after she came back into his life. Did I think I could ignore it? Stop it? Now that we were having the conversation, the genie was out of the bottle.

Danny moved to sit next to me, and his thigh pressed into mine. "What I want from her doesn't make me want you any less."

Why couldn't he have at least *tried* to deny how much he wanted her? But why would he at this point?

"I won't give you up for her," Danny said.

That was true. I heard his honesty. This was a moment where everything changed, based on what I did and said and decided to do next.

Responsible Brandon said it was time to stop screwing around with Reese. I needed to dial things back with her, and do everything I could to keep Danny here. The two of us were good together.

Then there was Reckless Brandon, who was tired of being kept on a leash. Who was burned out at work, and felt my soul spark to life every time I made what Responsible Brandon considered a bad decision. Reckless Brandon wanted to say *fuck it*, and have more Reese, and even see Danny with Reese.

Could I do that? Could I watch the two of them together? Danny had only been teasing her today. Not touching her—it was all words. I was torn between remembering how much Reese hurt Danny and seeing how good it had felt to just *do* these last few days.

"What do we do next?" Danny asked.

It was an open-ended question. He meant in regard to Reese, but I didn't have that answer. I was so tired of being responsible, I couldn't even confront my own emotions. Instead, I knocked Danny back on the bed, and straddled his waist. "Next, I do you."

"This isn't a solution." Danny worked his hips against me, despite the words.

"It's not-not-a-solution," I countered.

He gave me a skeptical smile. "I can't think of an argument."

And I was tired of thinking in general. I crashed my mouth down on his, swallowing his groan and molding our bodies together as tightly as possible.

Danny was hard against my hip. I needed to feel more. I pulled away enough to strip off his shorts, and his cock sprung free. When I gripped his shaft, he bucked into my touch with the kind of moan that lit up my senses.

I wasn't up for foreplay or dragging this moment out—I needed to feel him wrapped around me now. I hated to break contact even long enough to grab the lube, but some necessities couldn't be ignored. In short order I returned, knelt between his legs, and freed my cock.

I stroked him while I glided lube along his ass and teased his entrance with a finger. As he fell into the physical, his eyes half closed, his mouth slightly open in an unfinished sigh, I squeezed his shaft harder. Pumped faster. Dipped a finger inside him.

When Danny was panting, his hips bucking with each pump I eased up

He opened a single eye and watched me with wary amusement. "Tease."

"Not so much." I pressed against his hole with the head of my cock.

His groan stretched out as he did, and mingled with mine, as I slid inside him. And then I was hammering hard and fast, gripping his dick again, and jerking him in time to the way I thrust inside him.

Danny's guttural cry when he came was familiar and electrifying and yanked me over a chasm of need. Climax built inside me, nudging, surging, clenching my balls until I plummeted into the depths of pleasure.

I spilled inside him, still slamming until I was spent and too tender to push anymore, then collapsed next to Danny on the bed. I pulled him into me, and kissed his shoulder. He was salty with perspiration and the scent of soap was still heavy on his skin.

This was bliss. This was perfection.

This was me trying to avoid thinking about reality.

The thought slammed into me and I shoved it

away, locking it into the back of my mind. Sometimes a guy needed to let go and lose himself in the man he loved. There was nothing wrong with that.

15 /
danny

I was almost always up for great sex. And as I lay in a nice bed that someone else would have to make, in the middle of the afternoon, with my boyfriend, I didn't have any regrets.

That thought was a problem though—why would I? Why should I?

Because Brandon initiated the entire thing to distract me—and probably him—from finishing our talk about Reese.

So the sex? That was great.

Brandon's reasons for it? Not so much.

"The earlier conversation isn't over." I hated to shatter any moment, but we had to finish what we started. I rolled up on one elbow to look at him.

He stared past me to the ceiling, instead. "I still don't have an answer."

I didn't want to do this, but if I didn't establish

the boundary now, I'd regret it when it was too late. "You can't go out and fuck whomever—Reese or otherwise—but put restrictions on me if I want to do the same." My therapist would be proud of me. That didn't give me any love for this moment, though.

"But this isn't just anyone, is it?" Brandon asked.

I rested a hand on his cheek and forced his gaze to mine. "No, she's not. At some point, you have to trust me."

"It's not you I don't trust."

"No?" I searched his face. "If I tell you I know what I'm doing, that this won't go with her like it did before, that I'm aware of where I'm stepping, and you bring up what she did to me in the past, that means you don't trust that I know all of that."

Brandon worked his jaw. "It's more than just sex between the two of you."

I was pretty sure at this point it was more than just sex between the two of them, but I wasn't sure if it was adoration driving Brandon or something else. Especially after this afternoon. The realization sank like a pit in my gut. Something else was going on with him, and I couldn't define it. Or didn't want to.

I sighed. "If I had sex with Reese, yes it would mean more."

"But it already does," Brandon said.

I nodded. It was too late to shove that aside or pretend my falling for her again wasn't happening.

Brandon reached up and drew his thumb along my cheek. "If you're going to let me sleep with someone else, I won't put restrictions on you doing the same."

"Even Reese." I needed this to be clear. Stamped and signed off on and obvious.

"Even Reese."

"Even if you're not there." I didn't have any intention of that, but if we were negotiating, I was covering my bases.

Brandon worked his jaw.

"I'd expect the same for you," I said.

He furrowed his brow. "All right."

Should this feel like a victory? It didn't. Something was still off about the entire situation, but I'd pushed the issue about Reese and I wasn't taking it back. "We need to have this conversation with her, too. You do owe her a mall trip."

"All right."

The mall was safe. Public. Far less chance of fucking or random decisions to throw caution to the wind. I grabbed my phone and sent her a quick text. *Mall tomorrow?* The simple question ached with familiarity and longing. If she and I had this tech twenty-five years ago, our phones would've been filled with that same message.

The note popped as *Read*.

Three little animated dots appeared.

And nothing.

Given how she hurried out of here, I shouldn't be surprised. Maybe she was working, but I doubted it. What I wasn't sure of was if she was mad at me or something else. I couldn't watch my phone for hours. "Should we get breakfast? Lunch?"

"Yeah." Brandon grabbed the room service menu. "What are you in the mood for?"

For this tension to shatter and things to go back to what they were. Singing in shitty venues, watching Brandon decline because he was burning out, and pretending Reese and I were just friends.

Maybe I didn't want that. This uncertainty wasn't a great alternative, though. At least the status quo was familiar. "French toast?"

"On it." Brandon phoned in our order, and hung up. "Movies?"

When we'd made the hotel reservation, the plan was to indulge. Stay in the room through Sunday, do everything we wouldn't normally do, including paying too much for room service and pay per view movies.

It seemed silly now, but it also felt necessary. "What do they have?"

We landed on the latest superhero movie, and we watched the explosions while we fed each other

French toast and fresh strawberries. We logged back onto the game in the afternoon, did a raid with Jeremy and Nigel, and fucked around in some of the less populated areas.

We were fighting a big boss when my phone chimed with a new text. I forced myself to keep my attention on the game.

As we wrapped things up, sorted out loot, and left the dungeon, I tried not to fidget.

When we were back in town, Brandon handed me my phone. "You should probably look."

I pulled up Reese's reply. Her *sure* was hardly classic literature, but it was an answer.

Pick you up at noon, I sent back. There was no reason to go before that, the malls wouldn't be open. That didn't stop me from wanting to head to her place right now.

When we picked Reese up on Sunday, I had no idea how to broach the topic with her. I'd run a dozen scenarios in my mind, over and over, and none felt right. I was leaning toward the generic and frequently terrifying-to-be-on-the-receiving-end-of *so Brandon and I talked about you...*

"Hey-o." Reese's smile was warm but guarded as she slid into the back seat of Brandon's SUV.

Most people wouldn't notice the shift, but she might as well have screamed *things aren't right* at me.

"We talked, and it's okay if you fuck my boyfriend," Brandon said.

This was why people spoke in emoji. Why use words when a facepalm summed the situation up just as well?

Reese was silent. I had to twist in my seat to see her pursed lips and raised brows.

"But is it really?" she asked flatly.

No more wondering how to bring up the topic. Wonderful.

"Yes, it really is." Brandon's tone softened.

I watched Reese's face do the same. "If you're interested," I said.

One corner of her mouth tugged up. "I am." She frowned again. "Wait. Is this Brandon's way of getting out of going to the mall?"

He gave a short laugh. "No, but now I'm wishing I'd thought of that."

"Now that we have that out of the way, mall time." Reese announced.

It couldn't possibly be this easy, but if they were both being agreeable, I wasn't going to argue. In fact, if they said everything was fine, as far as I was concerned it was. I could go back to being who I wanted with Reese.

When we got to the mall, I offered Reese my arm. "M'lady."

"Thank you, good sir." She hooked her hand around my elbow. "I assume your man is prepared to carry our bags?"

I doubted Brandon appreciated the terminology, but the exchange with Reese was easy and comfortable.

As Brandon joined us, his mouth was set in a hard line. "*His man* is prepared for you to carry your own bags." A hint of teasing lay underneath.

"Because his man will be too laden with his own packages to help with mine?" Reese's voice was light as we walked toward the mall.

Brandon grabbed his crotch. "His man is already laden with a rather large package. But otherwise, unlikely."

I grinned. This was much better than yesterday. A nagging voice in the back of my mind still insisted *too easy*, but some things were. The three of us had grown a lot over the years, and now that we'd talked, life could move on.

As we drew closer to the building, where the crowds of people were denser and the Christmas music was audible and the scents of pine and cinnamon drifted through the air, Reese's smile grew. When we were teenagers, she loved the mall. She was going to be the next Debbie Gibson. When we'd hang out here, she had an entire plan.

"Where to first?" Brandon asked as we stepped inside.

Reese stared at him blankly, as if she didn't understand.

I slipped my free hand into Brandon's. "There's no list," I said. "We wander until we're done."

"It's almost like you're not a mall person." Reese steered the three of us like the pro she was, around other groups and individuals.

I already knew that about Brandon, but even after all these years it was weird to me that there were people who hadn't spent their teenage years living at the mall the way Reese and I did.

"Fine." Brandon's huff was exaggerated. "Show me how to do this mousy mall thing."

I snorted. "Mall rat?"

"Yeah. That."

"I think Danny already summed it up pretty well. We wander, we go into the shops that look neat, we eat cheap pizza, and if we're feeling rich we splurge on cookies and coffee drinks."

"So this is about overpriced mall food?" Brandon asked. "I'll buy you cookies if you want cookies."

I tugged them toward a shop with all sorts of novelty items. "Come on, Reverse Santa. Experiencing it is much different than hearing it explained."

"Mhm." Brandon didn't sound convinced, but he followed us anyway.

We made our way from store to store, and with

each new destination, Reese's mood brightened more.

A Christmas themed shop came into view as we rounded a corner, and Reese squealed. "There." I pointed.

Brandon's sigh was audible over the crowds.

"Come on, Scrooge." I pulled him along with us.

Brandon clucked. "I take exception to that. I have no problem spending money. I'm far more of a Grinch."

"You'd steal all the presents from the Whos down in Whoville?" Reese asked in mock horror.

Brandon rolled his eyes. "No. But I would rather stay at home with my puppy than sing carols with the crowds." He tugged the short strands of my hair enough to pull my head back and steal a kiss.

This was better than good. Reese was acting like herself, so was Brandon, and I was blissful between the two of them.

The Christmas shop was comfort wrapped in warmth. Gorgeous ornaments from around the world decorated trees and shelves, the entire place smelled faintly of cookies and coffee, and the music was tacky and delightful. I loved it all.

As we wandered through the displays, even Brandon stopped to admire some of the art and craftsmanship.

"Careful your heart doesn't melt," I teased.

He brushed his lips over mine again. "Too late."

Yup. Perfect.

Reese led us toward a display at the far end of the shop that featured a full-blown Christmas village. She'd always wanted a setup like this, but they were expensive and took up space. A few years ago, I'd tried to convince her to buy a house at a time, and leave the whole thing at our place, but she'd refused.

"Isn't it stunning?" Her smile hadn't faded since we got here.

"What lights them?" Brandon asked.

I picked up the nearest box and read the back. "Two AA batteries."

Brandon took the package from me and studied it. "They're not rechargeable or anything."

"The entire world doesn't run on USB." I set the piece back with the others.

Brandon shook his head. "Important thing to remember about batteries, but you both know it already."

I had a feeling Reese was thinking something very different than Brandon was. "What's that?" I asked.

"They die."

"Oh." Reese scowled. "That's totally not what I was thinking."

I laughed. Called it. "You were thinking about vibrators, weren't you?"

"Without question."

Brandon wandered away. "And now I'm going to be thinking about vibrators too."

"You're welcome." Reese blew a noisy kiss at the back of his head as she and I followed him out of the store.

"A person has to wonder—it's me, by the way, I'm that person—if you spent so much time here back in the day, how much dressing room sex did the two of you have?" Brandon asked.

Yup, things were back to normal. "With each other, none. We weren't dating back then."

"Besides, dressing room sex is a pain in the ass, and not in a good way," Reese added.

Brandon shook his head. "She said from experience."

We wove around a group of three mothers with strollers, walking side by side.

"Have you tried on a lot of clothes in the mall?" Reese asked.

I laughed.

Brandon shook his head. "As few as possible."

"Most of the places that sold clothes for teenagers had problems with security." Reese paused to take in the Christmas display in front of one of the shops. "Admittance to the rooms was closely monitored, and some of them didn't even have doors."

She had a point, but I hadn't completely abstained from mall sex when I was younger. "Bathrooms and storage closets tucked away down side halls were much better for getting nasty in."

Reese snorted. "You were such a slut back then."

"And I'm not ashamed to admit it now." I grinned.

"Whoa." Brandon held up a hand. "You're serious."

Why wouldn't I be? "Yes?"

"And you've never mentioned this before." His tone was unreadable.

"It's a part of my past I don't live in much." We both had sexual partners before each other, and while we didn't keep our history a secret, we didn't discuss details either. "Does it matter?"

"Eh." Brandon's grunt was noncommittal. "It means we would've come to the mall a lot sooner."

Fair point.

"Danny." Reese grabbed my arm and spun me in a new direction. "They have a piano."

Right at the edge of the food court, boxed in on three sides with Christmas decorations. A sign next to the baby grand listed when live performances would be over the next few weeks.

Now wasn't on the list.

"No shit." *God* that brought back some good memories. Better than janitor closet sex for sure. "Should we?"

"Maybe." Reese's reply was a lot more like *well duh* than *I don't think so*.

Brandon looked between the two of us. "Want to fill me in?"

Reese clucked. "It's easier to show you. Stand back and enjoy the show."

"What show? What are the two of you up to?" Brandon's question landed against our backs.

I approached the keyboard first, and plucked out a few tentative notes. The opening chords to *Carol of the Bells*. The shoppers nearest me glanced in my direction, but most everyone ignored me. My hesitation was an act that built into confidence as I tapped at more keys, and then flowed into the music.

I'd played this song enough times I could keep half an eye on the building crowd. Without looking, I knew Reese was edging closer, with a similar feigned hesitation to when I'd started playing. She was waiting for a cue only we knew was coming.

When I hit that point, Reese was close enough to strike a few keys in the higher ranges.

I never paused.

She slid into a few more bars.

This was dangerous. Technically it violated Reese's contract. But she was already in trouble and this was a lot of fun. Within a few seconds, the two of us were playing a full duet, pounding the keys with ease and fluidity.

I rose from the bench, still playing. That was Reese's next cue. We moved toward each other and swapped places, her sitting and me standing, the song never stopping.

It was so easy to lose myself in the music. Every time I played with Reese it was like this. It was why I didn't care what kind of crowds we drew as a band —I was there for the performance and the synchronicity with her.

Disappointment twinged inside as we neared the end of the song, but I'd rather appreciate that we got to do this at all.

We finished, and there was a heartbeat of silence before applause broke out around us.

Reese had to be devouring that, and I couldn't stop grinning. We stood and took a bow in each direction, and finished by facing each other.

Instinct and memories kept the show going as she grasped my fingers, stepped in, and pressed her lips to mine.

Exactly the way we used to. To an even louder round of applause. I leaned into the kiss, relishing her moan and that no one would hear it but me. She traced her tongue along the seam of my lips. Sparks threatened to consume us as heat flooded my body.

This was the chemistry I'd told myself for years was gone. The need I'd tried to bury under *we're just friends*.

And now I didn't have to stop. There was no going back from this. I cared about Reese as much as I always had. My entire world had just changed.

16 /
reese

I didn't deserve this. I didn't deserve Danny. But the instant his mouth met mine, it was impossible to pull away.

If we stayed here, I'd shove him back onto the piano bench to find out just how okay Brandon was with me fucking his boyfriend, and I didn't care how many of these people saw.

I broke away from Danny with a gasp. "I think I'm done shopping."

"Me too." He tangled fingers with mine as if it were the most natural thing in the world.

Brandon fell into step with us. There wasn't any conversation as we left the mall behind and headed out to the parking lot.

I was surprised when Danny opened the front passenger door rather than getting the back door first, especially when he slid into the seat.

He tugged my hand. "I want you on my lap."

That was ridiculous, and I was absolutely doing it.

"I'm pretty sure that's not completely safe." Brandon climbed into the driver's side.

"Do you want me to move?" I squirmed against Danny, and he gripped my hips.

Brandon started the vehicle in response.

Danny and I toed that line between friendly and more, but there was always the unspoken agreement we weren't more. It never left my mind that he was with Brandon.

With the door open, it was so easy to cross that line. To let my mind tumble into remembering his touch and his kisses and how he felt against me and inside me. It didn't matter that it had been more than a decade—the only thing that meant was we were both more experienced.

Danny slipped his hands under my shirt and glided his palms up my stomach. The heat was a shock compared to the cool air outside, and his light touch made my pulse hammer out a frantic beat.

I leaned more weight into Danny, and focused on his touch as he teased me through my bra. Could any of the cars around us tell what he was doing? I hoped so. Brandon certainly could. The public-but-hidden display made need throb between my thighs.

There wasn't a lot of room to maneuver in here, but that didn't stop Danny from pressing the seam of my jeans into my pussy and rubbing enough to drive me wild. By the time we reached their place, I was breathless and wet with need.

The instant we were inside, before the door finished closing, Danny boxed me against the nearest wall, and kissed me again, teasing my tongue and laughing through groans when I nipped at his lips. He made quick work of the button and zipper on my jeans, and dragged my clothes down my legs.

I giggled through my own frustration when the clothing got caught on the top of my Docs. "Probably need to take my shoes off first."

"Stupid details." Danny's grumble was good-natured. He had to pull the denim up enough to unlace my boots. He slipped those off first, and the rest of my bottoms followed immediately after.

The frantic charge in the air was familiar, a call back to the first time, so many years ago, when we finally realized we were more than friends, and slept together for the first time.

There were so many times with him after, and the ones nearest our breaking up were bittersweet morsels in my mind.

This was all fresh and new again. I had a brand new understanding of Madonna's *Like a Virgin*.

Danny knelt in front of me and kissed along my stomach as he trailed his thumbs over my hips, along the creases of my legs, and down the inside of my thighs. He dropped his mouth, until his lips and hands reached the same spot.

I groaned in desperation when he teased along my slick skin. He licked a path toward my opening, parting my folds with his tongue then diving inside me.

Goddess I missed this. This connection with him. The spark that flowed between us with each intimate touch. And the way he went down on me. I'd definitely missed that.

Brandon gripped my chin, and twisted my head to his to claim my mouth. I gasped against his lips when Danny pressed his fingers into my clit. I needed something to hang onto. To dig my fingers into. I fisted Brandon's shirt and he moved a hand to my breast, to knead through clothing.

Pleasure built inside me, edging me further up the scale with each touch and kiss and grope. I dropped a hand to cup Brandon's cock, and he bucked against my touch. I might have smirked with self-satisfaction, but I was too wrapped up in how this all felt. Tasted. The sounds the three of us made.

My world dropped away when Danny hit the right spot and circled my swollen button hard and fast. I plummeted into orgasm, grinding against Danny's face, holding onto Brandon's shirt as if nothing else could keep me here.

When my body jerked away with too much stimulation, Danny eased up. I leaned against the wall, laughing lightly through gasps for breath. "Fucking hell, I missed that," I muttered.

"Me too." Danny's amusement was audible and mixed with a husky need.

I wanted more. I looked down to see him still on his knees, watching me with an adoration that made my heart pause.

Brandon rested his lips against the hollow behind my ear. "Bed?" His question hummed against my skin.

"Fuck yes." I reached for Danny, and he and Brandon leaned into me as we walked the short distance to their room.

I lost track of who was kissing whom, as we yanked off the rest of each other's clothes in frantic need to be closer.

When I lay on the bed, the hammering of my heart was to a whole new beat. This was different than when I'd been in here with Brandon. It was familiar but not. It was a moment I'd daydreamed of for years, and hated myself for doing so.

And now it was okay. It was more than okay. Everyone wanted it. I might suffocate without it.

Danny rolled on a condom and knelt between my legs. The way he searched my face made my breath catch. I wanted to say something. I wanted to say everything. And with this being a tentative next step, I didn't dare say anything.

He pushed my legs to my chest and glided the head of his cock along my pussy. When he slid inside me, in a single, smooth thrust, I arched into him until he was buried to the hilt.

Brandon joined us on the bed, and I rolled my head to watch him stroke himself.

I tapped his leg and motioned for him to move closer. He pressed the head of his cock to my mouth, and I opened hungrily to let him.

And then Danny was moving, a rapid build to a hard, fast pounding. He struck something inside me, both physically and emotionally, that was desire mixed with longing.

I tumbled into the sensations and emotions, not wanting to miss anything, but not able to process all of it. Release inched forward, surging on years of missing that last bit of connection. Of so desperately wanting more.

Brandon slipped in and out of my mouth as the movement became more frantic, but I wanted another taste, and another. I wanted them both. I wanted it all.

I hovered on the cusp of climax, until Danny's pounding sent orgasm spilling through me. I let myself sink into the sensations, losing myself in the pleasure. In this bond that I'd shattered but somehow magically had back again.

Brandon's grunts grew more punctuated. Louder. Harder.

Danny gripped my thighs and leaned into me with more pressure, groaning.

There was a stutter Brandon's voice, a pause, and then sticky, salty warmth spurted across my face and chest.

I recognized the sounds Danny made when he came. The drawn out groan that both teased and taunted me in dreams. He still pounded, but slowly, the intensity eased off, the edge softened, and then he stopped.

I didn't dare open my eyes. What if this all vanished? I had to hold onto this bliss for as long as I could.

There wasn't much conversation, but there were a lot of soft touches and smiling glances as we cleaned up, and then the three of us collapsed on the bed together.

I was wrapped up in Danny and he was wrapped up in Brandon and this was perfect. Now that I'd had this taste, I couldn't let Danny go again.

"Is this just sex?" If the answer was *yes*, what would I do? I couldn't shove this feeling back inside.

"No. It's more." Danny's voice was soft, but the words roared with comfort in my mind. "I don't know what, but how could it not be more?"

It was weird having this conversation in front of Brandon, but it also made sense. There was more with him, too. Not the same as I felt for Danny, and not the same kind of potency I'd go to extremes to keep, but there was something with Brandon.

I curled tighter into Danny. "We don't have to define it yet, as long as it's something." I wasn't going to fuck things up with him this time. If I could have him, I was going to hold onto him for as long as I could.

After we'd refilled on cuddles, Brandon suggested we fiddle around in the music room, but that reminded me of the potential dread that awaited tomorrow. Instead, we spent the rest of the day doing a lot of nothing. It was incredible.

As night crept up then overwhelmed us, we decided I'd rather sleep here. One of them would drop me off at home on their way to work.

I was almost asleep, loving being so close to Danny still, when Brandon climbed out of bed.

He gave Danny a quick kiss. "I'll be back in a bit," he whispered.

Danny's expression wilted ever so slightly.

"Is it something I did? Is it me being here?" I asked softly when Brandon was gone.

Danny shook his head. "No. But an artist takes inspiration when it happens, right?"

Fair point. I curled up with Danny again and dozed off.

When the bed shifted with someone climbing into it, waking me up again, the clock on the night-stand said it was almost two in the morning.

Brandon wrapped himself around Danny without a word. Despite Danny never opening his eyes, the shift in his breathing said he'd woken up too.

The entire situation felt off, but sleep lulled me in again before I could think about it too much.

The next morning, I got up when Danny did, and Brandon slept through all of it.

Danny shook him awake, and Brandon fixed him with a wicked glare, through half-closed eyes.

"I'll make coffee. Don't go back to sleep. See you in the office?" Danny said.

Brandon pulled a pillow over his face. "Sure."

Definitely *off*.

But I got to wake up with Danny. I couldn't think of anything that felt more right. As we headed toward the kitchen, I pinched his butt.

He yelped and swatted playfully at my hand. "What was that for?"

"I had to make sure I wasn't dreaming."

He grasped my wrist and kissed my fingertips. "Nope. It's real."

Every touch and kiss between his place and mine was just as vivid, and just as dreamlike. I was so fucking smitten. I wasn't going to fuck this up again. Nope. Nope. Nope.

Danny dropped me off at my place and promised to give me a call later. I headed inside, sang in the shower, and grabbed my phone to see if I could pick up any spare work for the day.

While I was scrolling through listings, someone knocked. I answered the door to find a man on the other side who was holding a clipboard. "Reese Ellis?"

"That's me."

He handed me a few stapled papers. "Have a nice day." He turned and left.

I barely needed to see the text up top to know Todd was making good on his threat to sue me. Sure enough, his name was in the *Plaintiff* box and I was the *Defendant*. At least Danny's name wasn't on here. I sent him a text letting him know he was in the clear.

His reply came through quickly. *Are you okay though?*

I'll be fine, I replied. This was my mess to clean up. That penance owed for a serious mistake.

Next up, I took scans of the legal complaint and emailed them to Josh Hunter. He was a lawyer I'd met at a free legal clinic the city offered. He was only supposed to answer questions during the clinic time, but he tended to be available for me whenever I needed to talk about my contract.

It sucked that he couldn't do more than answer questions, like take my case, but I didn't expect anyone to work for free.

I was useless for the few hours his reply took, even though I had a good idea of what he would say. Even though I wasn't responsible for the video that was posted, I'd violated my contract by performing at the Christmas party.

Josh's reply confirmed my fears. He told me what to write in my official response, and warned me that if there was a lot of back and forth, I would need legal representation. If Todd pushed the issue too hard, this could cost me upwards of one-hundred thousand dollars or more.

I'm sorry I can't do more for you, Josh wrote at the end of the email.

It wasn't his fault any more than it was Danny's. It wasn't anyone's fault but my own.

And Todd's. Fucking Todd.

17 /
brandon

Adam knocking on the bedroom door, calling, "Hey, you up?" dragged me from sleep.

I groaned and forced my eyes open, but that didn't mean they wanted to focus. The *9* on the clock made me groan louder. *Fuck*, I'd fallen back asleep after Danny woke me up.

"Yeah, I'm here." I pushed out the words and made myself sit. Stumbling to my feet was next, and I shook away more of the haze of sleep as I reached the door and opened it. "What's up?"

Adam handed me his phone. "It's for you."

Weird. "Hello?"

"You went back to sleep, didn't you?" Danny's question was light rather than accusing.

I huffed out a sigh and scrubbed my face. "Apparently."

"I told Judith you were sleeping off a headache

and you'd be in a little later. You still good to come to work?"

This was weird, having him call me from my office. Not that I was complaining since he'd provided my excuse. "I'm good. Be there as soon as I can. Love you."

"Love you too."

I hung up and went to hand Adam back his phone, but he was already gone. I fumbled my way through getting ready for work. Definitely wasn't cut out for long nights and early mornings, but yesterday was worth it—both the afternoon and the inspiration that hit last night.

Adam was working at the kitchen table, like every work day morning last week.

I slid him his phone. "How goes it?"

"Not great, but I'm working on a plan."

I hid my eyeroll. He was always working on a plan. Until he found a better plan. "So the manufacturing and design idea is gone?" I asked.

"No." He looked at me with a frown. "That's the plan. Just because the workshop is gone doesn't mean I've given up."

"Oh. Okay." That was new for him. I grabbed the coffee pot, did some basic math, and set it back down. "Is this fresh?"

"Depends on what you mean by *fresh*. Danny made it a few hours ago."

Which explained why the pot was cold. Fuck. I'd grab something on the way to the office.

Traffic was light this late in the morning, something to be grateful for, and I was more awake by the time I reached the building where AcesPlayed was located.

The moment I stepped through the front door, Ivan—our office manager and Judith's assistant—stopped me. "Boss wants to see you."

A lot of people didn't like that phrase, but it had never meant bad news for me. Walking in two hours late might change that statistic. "When?"

"She said as soon as you got in. She's not in a meeting right now, want me to tell her you're on your way?"

"Sure." Why the fuck not. I bypassed the music room and headed to the far corner of the floor where Judith's office was. She had the only view in the place, and it wasn't a great one, but she'd earned it.

She looked up when I knocked on the doorframe, and motioned for me to come in. "Close the door."

I let it swing shut behind me and took a seat across from her. With another drag of too-hot coffee, I was ready for conversation. "What's up?"

"How's the headache?"

The... Oh, right. "Better, thanks." I held up my coffee cup. "Caffeine makes the world go round."

"That's a truth. So, Friday night, the Christmas party."

"It was awesome?" I had no idea from her tone where this was going.

She nodded. "Also a truth. Reese and Danny... Tell me why you've never collaborated with them."

"I have?"

"For work. For us. A friend's son watches these videos with people singing to video game music. Can we do that? With them?"

Not where I expected this to go at all. It didn't change my answer, though. Or rather, Reese's answer. "No."

"Why not?" Judith frowned. "You've got that recording of them here, singing to your song. Danny's lyrics. You always tell me *contract issues*. Phillip told me the same. What kind of contract?"

"The shitty kind." I didn't need to mince words with Judith.

She gave a short laugh. "I gathered. Details?"

"That's the problem—there aren't many. The contract says Reese's manager owns all of her performances, in all formats, for all venues. And that if she violates that clause, she's responsible for damages."

"Ouch." Judith sucked in a sharp breath through her teeth. "No clauses for ending the contract?"

"Manager can set a buy-out amount. As far as I

know, Todd's given her a ridiculous one." Speaking of, I needed to find out if she was served this morning. If he'd made good on his threat.

Judith leaned back in her chair, studying me. Silence ticked away in the room, and I downed more coffee.

Definitely no more late-night composing for me.

She finally straightened up again. "What if I could put her in touch with someone who could get her out of the contract?"

"I assume there are a lot of people like that. She's gotten quotes, and it's expensive. She's not going to take hand-outs, either."

Judith furrowed her brow. "He'd do it as a favor to me, and I'd do it as a favor for her. No money changes hands."

"Why? I mean, don't get me wrong, you'd have her gratitude and mine, but…"

"I want them playing with you."

I grinned. "They're already playing with me."

"TMI." She rolled her eyes. "For game promo. I don't care what else they do, but I've got a feeling about them, and I want their voices attached to our brand."

"Same." I'd love that. Danny and Reese deserved so much better than crappy venues, and I couldn't guarantee it, but I was pretty sure if Reese was free of her contract, she'd be happy to do some promo spots with us.

"Don't say anything until I talk to Xander. I'd hate to get hopes up, but I'll let you know."

I stood. "Of course. Thank you."

I took the long route to the Music room, stopping by Luna's office to say good morning to Danny.

"Glad you made it. Feeling better?" he asked when I gave him a kiss.

I wasn't too fond of the *I had a headache* excuse, but I could play along for the day and it was my own fault for oversleeping. "I am. Did I miss anything?"

"Todd is suing Reese." Danny sounded irritated.

I didn't blame Danny for being annoyed. Judith's news flew to the tip of my tongue, and I swallowed it. I didn't like lying to Danny. After work, I'd tell him and make him promise not to tell Reese. Was that possible? "We'll figure it out," I said with more confidence than I'd had about the situation, well, ever.

The way Luna was watching me, expression disturbingly blank for her, was curious. "What's up?" I asked her.

She shook her head. "Nothing. Shoo, so we can work."

"Yes ma'am." I gave her a sloppy salute and headed to my own work area.

As the day wore on, my mood faded, consumed by creating and selecting the perfect footsteps, snowfall sounds, and street background noise. I should have stayed late, to make up for this morning, but when five rolled around, I was done.

I hung out a little longer anyway, trying to at least look like I wanted to be here, and then I was gone.

Monday nights meant band practice, though. Yes, I was tired of making noise all day and wanted to go home to more noise. Sound effects were a different universe than listening to Danny and Reese play, though.

The thought made me half hard. Weird reaction, and a bit awkward while I was walking to my SUV. The parking lot was half full, I was surrounded by workaholics, but Danny's car was already gone.

When I got home, Adam was still at the kitchen table—though probably *again* would be more appropriate. He couldn't have been there all day. Danny was working with him on something.

"No Reese?" I asked.

Danny frowned. "She says there's no point in practice if we can't play." His concern was tangible.

Now I really needed to be able to share what I'd talked about with Judith. I grabbed Danny and tugged him into another room. As I shared the conversation from this morning, some of his gloom lifted.

"There's a catch," I said.

"Of course there is."

"You can't tell Reese until Judith has more concrete information. I wasn't even supposed to tell you but how was I going to keep anything from you? Especially something so big."

"It's okay." Danny's smile didn't fade. "I can give Reese a little hope without spilling the beans."

Good. I didn't like the thought that she might feel even a little bit defeated. A *what's the point* wasn't like her.

As I thought about brightening Reese's day, it warmed me from the inside out. I was okay with her and Danny together. The thought felt right. I liked the way he lit up when she was around. It was true, I liked fucking her too.

Danny called Reese and told her he had a lead on helping with her contract, but he couldn't say more yet. She'd already made work plans for the night, but she promised to come over tomorrow instead. The way he brightened was worth a lot.

It was still early for their relationship, at least in this way. If it looked like Danny was slipping, or that she might hurt him, I'd step in, but for now, I looked forward to what happened next between the three of us.

Tuesday, I was excited to mix the new music I'd composed with the art team's replacement assets from the leak over Thanksgiving weekend. Most of the inspiration struck during those long nights, and it was some of the best work I'd done.

When I played it back for Phillip, his furrowed brows said he didn't share my enthusiasm.

"What's wrong?" I asked.

"Nothing. Just noticing it's a different tone than the last piece."

Of course it was. It was new and different and epic. "I decided to take things in a different direction. I didn't ask for your critique." The words snapped out harsher than I intended.

Phillip held up a finger. "Back the fuck up. It's not a critique, and you asked what I thought. I can give an actual critique if you want."

Dial it back. "No."

"We'll tweak the art to match, if this is the mood we're going for," Phillip said.

Fuck that. I'd give them the same old same old, like they expected. "Don't worry about it. Give me a few days to clean this up and I'll bring it back in line with what we always do."

"It's just a matter of tweaking lighting and a few outfits for my team."

"I've got it." Again, my reply came out more harshly than intended.

But I didn't. I stared at the keyboard most of the

day, plucked out a few notes here and there, but nothing came to me. Why was this environment so stifling? What was wrong with me?

Danny was only in the office half a day, because he had work in the afternoon, and when I got home, he and Reese were already practicing. They looked good together, but it was best when I slid in on the piano and joined them.

Correction, the sex after was better.

And as I left them to sleep, and went to fix Phillip's problem with my music, my creativity was on fire.

18 /
danny

Wednesday morning, I sent Reese on her way with a happy kiss, and made sure Brandon actually got out of bed, despite his growling.

By the end of the week, the pattern was obvious. Sex where Reese was involved equaled late nights of creating.

At best she was his muse. At worst...

I didn't know. But he and I needed to talk. Preferably while he wasn't stumbling through the house and we weren't late for work. I'd take the chance to talk to him on the drive to the office, but I had a group session at the shelter this morning.

I wandered into the kitchen to find Brandon watching something over Adam's shoulder on his laptop. Neither of them was smiling, in fact their frowns were almost identical. "What's up?" I asked.

I stepped up next to Brandon so I could see.

The headline said *Police Stand-off with Sandy Man Ends in Shots Fired.*

What the fuck?

I scanned as much of the article as I could, given the small screen and the number of ads on the site, and gave up at too many words offering too little information.

Adam clicked *Play* on the attached video, and cranked the sound up instead.

I listened in fascination and horror as the news anchor in a generic suit and a flat expression explained how the police had gone to arrest someone last night who was suspected of a fire in a downtown location.

I knew the address—it was Adam's workshop.

And the picture they flashed on the screen was Adam's business partner.

He'd opened fire on the police, but apparently they managed to take him into custody without anyone getting killed.

No. Seriously. What the actual fuck?

"This is fucked up, even for you," Brandon muttered.

Adam slapped the lid shut on his laptop and twisted in his seat. "Did you just blame me for this?"

"What? No." Brandon gave him a confused look. "I'm just saying—"

"You've been *just saying* a lot of nothing since I got here, and I don't know why. Is the passive aggressive bullshit because you want me to leave?" Adam asked. "Am I intruding on Brandon's Magical Manic Boinking Time?"

The phrase would've made me snicker if the tension in the room hadn't just cranked to a breaking point.

Brandon stared at Adam. "I'm not accusing you of anything, and if I said you can stay here, you're welcome to stay here. But you don't have the best track record. That's not me mincing words, it's the truth. This casualty for your current big plan is just more obvious than most of the distractions you toss aside and move on from without a second thought."

And apparently we were doing this now.

Adam gave a strained laugh. "Not everyone knew what they wanted to be the instant they turned eighteen. You realize you had your future handed to you, don't you? Brandon the Perfect Prodigy? One of Rinslet's golden children."

"I work as hard as anyone at my fucking job." Brandon spoke through clenched teeth.

"So do I," Adam snapped. "Do you think I like being thirty-two and not knowing where my next paycheck is coming from? Just because I didn't opt to sell my soul to the corporate slog doesn't mean I'm not trying to do something with my life."

"Some of us had to sell our soul, to keep from leaning on the rest of the world and expecting them to carry our weight."

Brandon's phrasing stuck in my thoughts. Did he think he had done that? Surrendered something for his job? Did he think I expected him to carry my weight?

"Sometimes—"

"Stop." I cut Brandon off before this could deteriorate any further. He and Adam turned their irritated glares on me. "Stop before one of you says something you regret."

"Too late." Adam stood and grabbed his laptop. "I'll be out by the time you get home, and I'll remember that *you're always welcome here* is bullshit."

Damn it. "Adam."

"Let him leave." Brandon sounded regretful, but not as much as maybe he should.

I turned to him. "What was that?" I kept my tone sympathetic rather than accusing.

He raked his fingers through his hair. "Years of pent-up frustration."

"You all but said you sold your soul for your job. You implied it's draining the life out of you. Are you that miserable at work?"

"I'm a little stressed, but I'm dealing."

I clenched my jaw. "Don't bullshit me. Out of all of the people in the world I need honesty from…"

Brandon's sigh filtered through his fingers, and when he pulled his hand from his face, his exhaustion was stark. "I'm not bullshitting you." The fight had vanished from his voice.

"But the late nights. The strung-out days. Talk to me. What's going on?" If we were going to talk this through now, we were going to do it right. I'd call work if I had to. His and mine. "Do you need the day off? What?"

"A day off isn't going to make a difference. But I do want to talk," Brandon said. "Tonight?"

"Swear to me we'll have an actual conversation, and sort this out."

Brandon kissed me. "Cross my heart. Just you and me tonight, dinner, conversation, and a little bit of soul exposing. What little I have left." His smile was tight.

I didn't like his phrasing, but I'd take the rest. "Okay. It's a date."

I got to the office after lunch, and Brandon was in meetings so I didn't get to say *hello*, but his night was mine so that was okay.

Instead, I joined Luna in her office. We were done updating employee machines and Cole had gone back to his work, but she and I were still figuring out who tried to steal our assets, and making plans about how to keep it from happening again.

We'd stripped everything we could from the files that had been posted online, and were no closer to finding new information than a week ago.

Today I was going through any information we could find about the company who had posted the campaign. The site that had the data refused to share it with us without a court order, which I appreciated but was also frustrated by since it was AcesPlayed stolen property.

I scrolled through pages of search results that pointed to other businesses with similar names, social media pages that had nothing to do with this, and screen caps from the campaign itself. Words went into my brain but didn't stick, and I moved on.

Something clicked in my mind as I paged away from a site. What was that?

I backtracked to the page, and scanned it again. Nothing stood out, but I'd seen *something*.

There it was—a familiar company name, but why? "You ever hear of Vopax?"

Luna shook her head. "It's kind of a dumb name, though. It sounds like someone pulled it from a keyword generator."

That was true of a lot of businesses. I wouldn't dare say it aloud to anyone here, but AcesPlayed wasn't the most brilliant name either. Though, at least it made me think of games. Not naked MMOs, but games.

I tracked back through anything I'd done in the

last few days that might be connected to this. Fucked a bit. Gamed a bit. There was this morning's argument with Brandon and Adam.

I frowned, and pulled up the article Adam showed us this morning. There it was, buried in the list of things Richard Hedd was associated with. This was one of half a dozen companies that he was suspected of having ties to and using to defraud people.

Now I had a pretty good idea how our game assets got online. If Adam was on our network and loaned a device or password to Richard at any time…

"So, I know how the leak happened." Telling Luna would be easy.

Breaking the news to Brandon, after the fight this morning with Adam… I wasn't looking forward to the fallout from that.

19 /
reese

When Danny called, I couldn't help my smile. It hadn't taken any time at all for me to fall back into *we're together again.*

"Miss me already?" I answered with a teasing tone. It had only been a few hours since I left their place.

"Always when you're not here." Danny's voice was warm.

This was definitely too easy. Not that I minded. "You know where to find me if it's that bad."

His laugh was light, but the pause that came after weighed down the air. "That's why I'm calling."

"Don't do that to a girl. Don't lead with a vague statement like that." I couldn't joke, though I wanted to.

"No, it's not that bad." Danny's reassurance

came quickly. "I just need to cancel tonight's plans, not all plans indefinitely."

That was a little better. "Is everything all right?"

"I assume it will be. I need to figure out what's going on with Brandon."

I can help. As much as I wanted to believe my future with Danny was secure and completely figured out and set in stone, I was still a third wheel in some ways. Besides, I had a good idea what he was talking about and what if I was the problem? "I get it. See you tomorrow for RinCon setup, and let me know if I can do anything."

"Definitely. To both. Miss you." Danny disconnected.

It wasn't as good as *love you*, but he also didn't make me feel like that was off the table, so there was still hope. It was weird feeling any security about my future, but I liked it.

I spent most of the morning and into the afternoon on calls with Bambi and my other clients, and by the time I wrapped up the last appointment, I was ready to chill. Maybe watch cheesy Christmas movies until I was weepy and happy and full of warm fuzzies.

As I was wrapping up my billing and finishing all the admin work for the evening, Todd called. One of the last people I wanted to speak to. Ever. And I was happy to tell him so. "What?" I answered.

"Don't be like that, Reese." His tone was smoother and kinder than I'd heard in a long time. "I called to talk."

Bullshit. Especially in that tone. "To talk about why you won't let me out of this contract? Or maybe about how you recognize that video had nothing to do with you and you should drop this stupid lawsuit?"

"All of those things and more." He sounded polite, but I wasn't hearing any answers. "Let me buy you dinner."

The asshole undoubtedly owed me a lot of years of shorting me out of what the band was and could be earning, but I didn't trust him to buy me anything. I could do a face-to-face meeting, though. Less room for him to squirm away if we had an audience, and I had a few gift cards that clients had sent me for Christmas. "Dinner sounds great, but I'm fine with splitting the bill. How about Grumpy's?"

"Sounds fantastic. Meet you there at seven?"

Seven at night, with Christmas coming up fast, at one of the most popular sports bars in town? The place would be packed.

Sounded like the perfect setting to get into it with him. "I'll see you then."

I didn't like his change in tone, and I wished I could bring Danny and Brandon with me for backup, but they had their own thing to work out.

Time to pull up my big girl panties, and *talk* to Todd.

At least I didn't have to go in completely alone —I would wear my favorite ass-kicking Docs and the battered leather bomber jacket I'd borrowed from Danny almost two decades ago, that never made its way back to him.

I also called ahead and had them save us a table, so Todd wouldn't be able to use the excuse *It's too crowded, let's do this another time*. Was it too much to hope that he'd seen my response to his lawsuit, realized how ridiculous this whole thing was, and decided to drop the suit and maybe my contract?

My own delusion almost made me laugh.

When I got to Grumpy's, the line of people waiting spilled out onto the sidewalk, and so did the too-loud Christmas music. The lights and fake evergreen decorations clashed completely with the normal decor.

I love all of it. Maybe tonight I'd get my own Christmas miracle.

"Reese, hey." Todd joined me, a phony ass grin pasted on his smug face. "I was worried you might not show."

"Wouldn't miss it for anything." I could do fake, but I wouldn't do it for long. We made our way to the host podium, and Todd looked surprised when I gave them my name and we were shown to a table right away.

He littered the conversation with small talk about the weather and Christmas plans while we ordered drinks. As our waitress brought us the chips and salsa, I was trying to figure out the best way to say *what the hell is this* without him walking out.

"You ever been to Slingers?" Todd asked before I could form the words. "Old bar. Shut down a few years ago?"

Random, but I wanted to see where this went. "I used to love that place." Danny and I played their open mic nights, and sometimes even real shows.

"I was in there one night, years ago," Todd said. "There was this woman at the bar who was *wow*, stunning."

I did *not* want to hear about his conquests. But curiosity won out and I let him keep talking.

Todd studied me for a heartbeat. "I took the seat next to her, and we chatted a bit. She had this kind of sadness to her, but she was kind and intelligent. Great voice and body. We really hit it off. I was into the conversation and so was she—the connection was amazing and I could tell she was feeling it too."

I swallowed a yawn as well as the desire to ask *but was she really?*

"And then her boyfriend joined us." Todd's tone shifted toward hard. "Fucking guitar player of all things. How the fuck am I supposed to compete with a guitar player? And weird thing is, he had a jacket that looked almost exactly like yours."

177

Ice slid down my spine. He was talking about Danny. Which meant he was talking about me.

"And you didn't even remember me the next time we met." Todd fixed a frightening gaze on me.

Thank the goddess for public places, right? "I didn't flirt with anyone else when I was with Danny. He was my universe." There were few things I could say with more certainty.

"You *fucking liar*." Todd's reply was a low growl. It would be less scary if he was shouting, but he didn't want anyone else to hear him. "You led me on that night, and you don't even remember because you're such a whore—"

"Do not." I bit off the words. Like he was the first guy to feed me bullshit like this? "It's not my fault you confused kindness with a pick-up."

"Then you do remember."

I shook my head. "I remember who I was and I know who I am. I've made a lot of mistakes, but any connection you saw was in your imagination."

"Bullshit." Todd's smugness was back. "You can't convince me of any of that, because I was there. I was also there when you dumped your precious guitar player the instant I offered you a solo deal."

Pieces slammed together in my mind, and an entire picture formed. Was he really— He hadn't— "You've strung me along for more than a decade because I wouldn't sleep with you?" No. That was so petty, it belonged in a TV movie.

"Not just you. Every bitch who ever pulled shit like that. You all deserve it, but you were the only one to take the bait. You selfish, self-centered—"

I stood and slammed my palms on the table, not caring that everything clattered and drew the attention of nearby tables. "You pathetic fucking asshole. I'll see you in court."

Todd grabbed my hand as I spun away, and yanked so hard I lost my balance and landed on the bench next to him. My skin crawled at the contact, and I struggled to break his grip.

"The offer is simple, gorgeous." He pressed his mouth to my ear and my stomach lurched. "Sleep with me, and I'll kill the contract. You were enough of a whore to leave for fame, and you can be a whore one more time and fuck me."

I yanked free and stumbled back a few steps. I didn't care who was watching us. "Keep your filthy dick away from me." I spoke loud enough the entire section would hear. "Anything else you have to say to me can go through my lawyer, whose information will be in my next complaint response."

I turned and stalked out of the restaurant, and was halfway to my car when my phone buzzed with a text from Todd.

We both know you can't afford a lawyer. Offer stands.

"Fuck you." I screamed at the screen before jamming the device in my purse.

This was real. This was actually happening. I'd been hit on and groped and worse by my share of creepers, but this...

And it didn't matter, because I was still stuck in this shitty contract, working with him.

20 /
brandon

I was coming unhinged. My mind was in tatters, at that point between the high of inspiration and the crash of exhaustion the next morning.

I was falling apart and I needed to pull myself back together. Going off on Adam this morning was a mistake. The last thing I wanted was to push him out of my life, regardless of the past. Regardless of the different ways we approached life, I'd never forgive myself if I lost Adam. If I let the same thing happen to him that happened to our father.

That thought was fixed in my mind as Danny told me Adam was indirectly responsible for our company assets being stolen.

No, that wasn't right—the responsibility lay with me. I'd given Adam access, and that made this my fault. I'd wasted more than a week of Luna's time. Danny's. Cole's. Phillip's. I'd cost the company money we shouldn't have had to spend. This was on me.

I assured Danny I was fine, and forced my way through the rest of the work day.

When I got home, Danny was already there, but Adam was gone. I sent my brother a quick message on my way into the house. *Let me know where you wound up, or come back here. You're still welcome here.*

Inside, I found Danny in the kitchen, and greeted him with a long kiss.

"I missed you too." He smiled against my lips.

Sanity seeped in from the simple act of touching him. Holding him. I needed to hang on to this feeling, because at this moment, all was right with the world. I sniffed the air. "Something smells good. In addition to you."

"Pad Thai." Danny pointed at the takeout bags on the table. "I figured if someone else cooked, we could get down to the important stuff."

"You're a genius and I love you for it."

He grinned. That warm, familiar, genuine Danny grin. "And here I thought you loved me for my big dick."

"That doesn't hurt." I considered my words. "I mean, sometimes it does, but that's part of the fun."

"Food and conversation first, and then we can make sex jokes."

I grabbed the bags. "You started it."

"And I'm hoping you'll finish it." Danny followed me into the living room. "Just not yet."

We settled into our favorite spots next to each other on the sofa, laid out dinner within reach on the coffee table, and picked at our food.

So much for talking. "Where do you want to start?" I asked.

"I was hoping you'd know that."

I dug through my brain. There were a lot of little things—Adam, the burn out, the snapping at my colleagues—but I wasn't sure which one he was bothered by.

"Do you want to stop seeing Reese?" Danny's question jarred me out of my head. "Do you want me to stop seeing her? Hanging out with her? Is her being here a problem?"

"What?" I didn't try to hide my confusion. "Definitely not. Why would you go there?"

Danny set his food aside. "Every time you're with her, you vanish after. You don't sleep in the same bed as her. As me. I thought it was a whim the first time or two, but it's impacting your work. Your moods."

"No." As I grasped Danny's meaning, I needed to assure him it wasn't true. "I promise, no. It's the opposite. The three of us together, we're incredible. The music. The sex. It's a kind of inspiration I haven't felt in a while, and when it hits, I don't want to lose it."

Danny's expression softened and his shoulders slumped. "There's got to be a better way."

"If there was, I'd be doing it." The snap came out without thought. "I'm sorry, that wasn't right."

"This is what I'm talking about, though. You're not you."

I didn't want to pick a fight with Danny. "You know work has me burned out. This helps me forget."

"You don't have to stay at this job."

I stared at Danny as if he'd grown two heads. Of all the people to suggest such a thing. After Reese pushed him away, I figured he'd understand how important it was to push through a problem. "It's just a little stress."

"It's just a little unhinged." He winced. "You can leave. No one will think less of you."

Unhinged. The same word that haunted me. That *taunted* me. "I'll push through it."

"I don't doubt that you can. But you don't have to."

"Yes, I do." My retort came out loudly. "I don't give up on something because it gets difficult. Not work. Not composing." Not life. I wasn't my father.

Danny's frown deepened. "You have to know this isn't working. Something needs to change."

"You're right." Part of me wanted to keep arguing, but it would be for the sake of feeling, and not because it would help. "I don't want to send Reese away." The words hit harder than I expected. The idea of a Reese-shaped void in our lives was foreign and disconcerting. When did that happen? "I'll make a conscious effort to tone down the... What did Adam call it?"

"Brandon's Magical Manic Boinking Time."

I twisted my mouth in mild frustration that Danny summoned the phrase so easily. "Let's keep the boinking, but I'll temper the mania after."

"I'm not asking you to ignore the bursts of inspiration," Danny said. "Just to find the balance between those and life."

"I will." Because that was what I did. I made the pieces work, and this would be no different. Besides, he was right—my behavior had changed and I didn't like being *unhinged*. "Are you good? Are we?"

Danny nodded with a soft smile. "Yes."

"Good." I made sure all the food was out of the way, knelt next to Danny, and cradled his face between my hands. "Dinner can wait. Let me make the bad behavior up to you." I needed to feel him. To ground myself in him.

He quirked an eyebrow. "If you insist."

I pushed Danny back and crawled up his body, shoving his shirt out of the way and kissing up his chest. His skin was hot against mine, drawing me in and cranking my need. I bit playfully along his skin and dragged my tongue over a nipple, pausing to tease the nub until he was breathless.

When my mouth finally met his, I fell into him. I was hard with desperation. I wanted more of him. To prove to him how good we were together. How much he meant to me.

I dragged down his zipper, and freed him. His hot cock jerked against my touch, and he let out a stuttered laugh when I dragged my thumb over the head. I slid back down his frame, and drew my tongue along the same path as my hand.

I took Danny in my mouth, and slid down his length in time with his drawn-out groan. I knew which buttons to push, how fast to stroke and squeeze, how to lick and suck, to get the right reactions from him.

He was beautiful, half reclined, watching me with lust and adoration, as I worshipped his cock. My own strained with need against my slacks, but I had to show him how much this mattered. How much he mattered.

I had to lose myself in him before I just lost myself.

His hips bucked and he fucked my face, and I sucked harder. Stroked faster. Lost myself in the abandon of tasting him. When his fingers tightened in my hair, I knew he was close. I fingered his sac, feeling it tighten under my touch, feeling his whole body tense beneath me.

A salty spurt hit the back of my throat, and then another, and I swallowed him until he was spent.

Danny relaxed back against the cushions with a shuddering sigh. I moved back up to kiss him, and he accepted hungrily.

Our mouths crushed together and our tongues danced. He undid my pants, and when he worked my cock free, a long, needy groan tore from my chest.

I was already so close, thanks to getting him off, and it didn't take much of Danny's coaxing to draw me to the edge of the cliff. He kissed me again, hungry and hard, and murmured, "I do love you," against my lips.

My chest clenched, my body tensed, and orgasm filled and flooded me, spilling out as he fisted me and pumped.

He slowed to a stop, and silence filled the room, not drowning out the ringing in my ears. My mind was silent. So blissfully quiet.

My pants were a sticky mess, but I didn't want to leave to change. Instead, we stripped out of all our clothes, wrapped ourselves in a blanket, each other, and not much else.

The food was lukewarm, but neither of us wanted to pull away long enough to heat it up. We sank into comfort while we ate and watched movies and sang along with the music and picked apart the dialog.

When we made it to bed, hours later, the peace we'd found turned to an itch in my mind. A nagging tune that wasn't quite there, but I knew I could grasp if I just had a keyboard in front of me.

After the conversation with Danny, the desire was obvious, and I knew the burst came from finding those few hours of peace with him. But it was more than that. It was the abandon. The recklessness that came with the messy, impromptu sex. The closeness. The ability to leave the outside world behind for a few hours.

I wouldn't indulge. Tonight my time was Danny's. We climbed into bed, and I held him while his breathing evened out, and he drifted off to sleep.

I couldn't do the same. I wanted to. But I also wanted to pull away and go indulge this need to build something new and wild. The longer I fought the urge, the more it clawed at my thoughts, until I was stuck in a loop of four bars, playing over and over in my mind, waiting for me to make them real so the next bits would happen.

The thoughts were almost maddening. What was going on with me?

21 /
reese

I tossed and turned most of the night, replaying Todd's twisted confession and demands in my mind until I wanted to scream. Had I ever been this furious before? Not in this way. This was a searing kind of white-hot rage.

Under it all, lay the whispers of blame. Not for leading Todd on—I hadn't done that and I knew it. But I had broken up the band and sent Danny away. Not for Todd's stupid contract, though that gave me the excuse. Yeah, I'd wanted the fame.

I'd also wanted to be hurt on my terms. If I made Danny leave, he couldn't decide to do it on his own later. Fate couldn't decide to take him from me.

I was an idiot who didn't deserve this second chance with him, but goddess I wanted it.

When I finally admitted that sleep wasn't happening, around five in the morning, I climbed out of bed. Something caught my attention out of the corner of my eye—an ornament box that I hadn't completely tucked away under the bed.

Instead of pushing it out of sight, I pulled it into view. Inside was a smaller box. One I ignored every year, out of habit more than anything at this point in my life. My chest tightened at the reminder of what was inside. For the first time in more than a decade, I opened the box.

The ornament was old, and far more intricate and expensive looking than anything I owned. It had been a gift from Danny's parents on my eighteenth birthday. The gilded, delicate angel had a photo in the middle.

Of me and Mom.

Something inside me cracked, and I couldn't pull my gaze away. Instead, I traced my thumb over the photo. "Hey, Mom. I missed you."

It was weird speaking the words aloud, but it felt good. It also hurt like hell, but in a *don't stop now* kind of way.

"It's been a long time, I know. I'm sorry about that." I had no idea if her ghost or angel could hear me. But if anyone's mother was watching over them from beyond, mine was.

"It's been a crazy few years." Despite the raw feeling in my throat, I wanted to tell her all about what she'd missed. The way I used to when I'd visit her in hospice. But this time there were years to catch her up on. "I've had some really big fuck-ups, and some amazing breaks, and goddess, Mom, I wish you were here to share it with."

Now that I was talking, I couldn't stop. I told her about the last fifteen years. About pushing Danny away. Breaking up the band. The stupid decision I made to sign my career away to Todd. I told her about getting Danny back, and meeting Brandon. All the wacky people he worked with. Adrienne. Luna. Everyone.

"I wish I could sing with you, one last time." I talked through tears and sniffles. "I miss you so much." The ache in my chest was massive, a pain I'd ignored for so long, but as I hung the ornament with the others, on the tiny tree in the corner, my soul didn't feel as heavy.

A knock on the door startled me. Shit, it was after nine. Had I really talked for that long? It would be Danny and Brandon.

I sniffled softly and dragged the back of my hand across my cheeks. A useless endeavor that didn't do anything but smear tears and snot across my face and wrist. "Hang on," I called. I hurried into the bathroom, splashed enough cold water on my face and hands to wash them clean, and blew my nose.

When I opened the door, seeing Danny and Brandon on the other side almost made me cry again as it tugged up the memories I'd just shared. I smiled instead. "Hey. Morning."

Danny ran his thumb across my cheek, and a shiver of comfort tugged at my tender heart. "You've been crying," he said softly.

I stepped aside enough to nod at the ornament. "I unwrapped that. It's been a while. I was talking to Mom, but I'm okay now."

"Was it a good conversation?" His question was pure kindness.

I nodded. "Yeah. It really was."

Brandon handed me a to go cup of coffee. "You still free today?"

"I am." The longer I talked to them, the more normalcy flowed in, mingling with old scars and feeling right. "Does the fact that you're both here, and look happy aside from some awkward shifting about, mean that you talked?" I wasn't going to beat around the bush about it; I needed to know they were better.

"We did." Brandon nodded. "Danny told me I was being a dick and I agreed to save the dickishness for fucking."

Danny chuckled. "It didn't quite happen that way, but close enough."

This definitely felt right. I gestured down at the T-shirt and shorts I'd tried to sleep in. "I'm not ready yet, I'm sorry. Long night. Give me ten? Or I can meet you there."

"We can wait."

I let them in, got ready for my day in record

time, and we were on our way to the Salt Palace downtown.

"What kept you up?" Danny asked as Brandon drove.

The question triggered an avalanche, and the memories of last night plus fury roared back. "Dinner with Todd."

When Brandon met my gaze in the rearview mirror, eyebrow raised, I realized how the words sounded. "Eww. Not like that, though he was certainly hoping it would be."

As I told the story, Danny turned in his seat to watch, and his features twisted into a kind of anger I wasn't used to seeing with him. When I finished, his jaw was set and his expression hard.

"Want me to go introduce him to my fist?" Brandon's anger was tangible as well.

"I really really do." I wanted to do some introducing of my own. "But wait until the lawsuit is over? And then take pictures." Their support was nice, even if it didn't solve anything.

When we arrived, inside the convention center was quiet compared to the bedlam it would be tomorrow. Small packs of people cut deliberate paths toward their destinations, hauling suitcases, trolleys, and more. We stepped through an open pair of doors, into the main hall. Banners hung from the ceiling with numbers, but we didn't need to go too far. The AcesPlayed booth was near the front of everything.

Since Scott McAllister, one of the owners of Rinslet, was also a silent investor in AcesPlayed, the company had access to a few con benefits most people would pay through the nose for. He rarely tossed his name into things, because he didn't want his reputation to overshadow Aces, but he made sure they got good exposure.

Adrienne grinned and waved when she saw us. Sonya and Jeremy looked up from the computers they were setting up, gave us smiles and *hellos* and went back to work.

Adrienne bounded up to us. "Thank you. So glad you're here. Okay, so Dustin is in one of the presentation halls, he wants Brandon's help with lighting and sound. Danny is supposed to make sure the computers are all secure. Reese, you can help me."

"What are we doing?" I knew in the generic sense—we were setting up the booth and helping Brandon do a dry-run of his presentation. But everyone else had specific tasks.

"You're helping The High Priestess oversee the ritual, presumably." Sonya didn't look up from her work.

I looked between her and Adrienne. "High Priestess? You got a promotion. Congratulations," I teased.

Adrienne shrugged. "No one told me."

"The chosen one is always the last to know." Jeremy handed Sonya a bundle of cables.

She moved to the next computer in the setup. "And when Venus moves into retrograde, and chaos descends upon love and work, the summoning ceremony will be complete."

"What am I summoning?" Adrienne asked.

"Good press, incredible reviews, and Christmas bonuses, I hope." Jeremy moved to a new section of the booth, and grabbed a box.

I shook my head, but I was amused. "Pretty sure y'all've already nailed all three."

"All hail High Priestess Adrienne." Sonya made bowing motions and Jeremy joined her.

I already knew creatives were weird, but writers took strange and random to a whole new level of epically bizarre.

All of us spent the day setting up, watching Dustin and Brandon run through the announcements, and generally making sure the Aces booth was set for the show Monday morning.

It was dark when we finished, even though it wasn't even six. Danny, Brandon, and I hopped on the light rail and rode it a few blocks to Temple Square. It didn't matter that none of us were Mormon—at Christmastime, this was one of the most beautiful places to see in the valley.

As we wandered through the lit-up grounds,

nostalgia pinged inside me. Mom always let me believe these lights had been set up just for me.

The temperature dropped as we walked, and then the snow started to fall. I loved the way the lights looked through the big, fluffy flakes. I loved even more that I got to experience it all with my hand nestled in Danny's, and his in Brandon's.

We decided to head home before the snow got too heavy to drive in. Brandon's mood was softer than I'd seen in a few weeks. At their place, we watched Christmas movies and he even looked entertained by Frosty rather than annoyed. The Grinch was still his favorite, though.

The next morning I realized the house was down a person. "Did Adam find a new place to stay?" I asked as we were eating breakfast.

Brandon's scowl was like a crack in an illusion, but it vanished quickly. "He and I argued. He decided to stay with a friend."

"You need to go easier on him," I said.

There was the scowl again. Dark and heavy. "It turns out his business partner is the one who stole our assets. Because Adam gave him access to our network. That cost us days of work."

"Okay." I held up my hands in surrender. That still didn't sound like Adam's fault, but I wasn't in the mood to face Brandon's abrupt irritation. "I didn't realize."

"It's fine." Brandon bit off the words. His mask

was back, modified with a smile that didn't reach his eyes. "We should put up the tree."

Because that wasn't suspicious at all.

Danny pressed the inside of his wrist to Brandon's forehead. "Are you all right? Kidnapped by aliens maybe?" His teasing sounded forced.

Brandon's expression relaxed. "I'm not in the mood to be moody. Let's have fun instead."

"I'll never turn down a tree decorating party. You ask me in June, and I want to decorate the Christmas tree." I wasn't always in tune with other people's feelings, but Brandon was projecting pretty hard.

The mood in the house slid back toward happy as we pulled out the tree and strung up ornaments and lights.

We were in the middle of making popcorn to thread onto string when Brandon's phone rang.

"'S Dustin," he said to us before he answered with, "What's up?" As he listened, his irritated expression grew back until it was etched in stone. "I'll be there soon." His tone was as hard as his face.

I was learning to distrust any calls he got in the middle of our fun.

"What's wrong?" Danny asked.

Brandon shoved back from the table, and the chair legs scraped loudly on hardwood. "Something's wrong with the sound setup at the Salt Palace. I need to go help him fix it."

I understood not wanting to work during off hours, but I'd never seen Brandon this kind of pissed about work before. Especially with friends.

"Do you want company? Need help?" Danny asked.

"No. I'll be back in a few hours."

When Brandon left, Danny was frowning.

"Are you sure you talked things out?" I hated to ask, but someone had flipped a switch on Brandon and turned him into Mr. Hyde.

Danny shook his head. "We should finish the popcorn strand."

"Don't do that." I finally had him back, and I wasn't letting go. "Don't shut me out."

Danny sank into his chair, and pulled me into his lap. "I don't know. He's burned out. He insists he can deal with it, and when he promises he'll try harder, what am I supposed to do? Call him a liar?"

I leaned my head on Danny's shoulder and pulled his arms around me. "No, but maybe also yes." Asking the next question hurt, because it reminded me of my own screw ups, but I needed to. "When you were recovering, after you met him, would he have called you on something like this?"

"He's not an addict."

"He's dealing with some pretty serious denial and internalizing a lot of stuff. I know you see the overlap."

Danny sighed. "I do. And he did. I had a hard

core relapse early in the relationship, and he told me he wouldn't watch me destroy myself."

We'd never talked about this part of his past before, and as much as I didn't want to hear about him hurting because of me, I needed to hear it, because it was part of who Danny was now. "What happened next?"

"I started the AA meetings and the therapy for him." Danny's voice was tight. "I couldn't stand the thought of being alone again."

A knot formed in my chest, and I swallowed my *I'm sorry*. It wasn't the right time.

"And it was so hard," Danny said. "Until my therapist chipped away at me enough to make me realize I needed to be getting better for me, and not out of the fear that he was going to leave me."

"I'm sorry I played a part in any of that." I couldn't hold the words back.

Danny kissed my nose. "I know you are. If you weren't, if I hadn't forgiven you, we wouldn't be here now. And I have forgiven you."

His words warmed me more than any happy Christmas feelings could. "What are you going to do about Brandon?"

"I don't know. Be there for him. Help him figure it out."

I wanted that. They were good together, and I didn't want to see Brandon and Danny fall apart. But, "Be careful with you, too."

"I will." Danny kissed me again, and nudged me into my own chair. "Popcorn string. Come on."

We finished hanging the Christmas ornaments, made hot chocolate, and watched more movies. It all felt right, except for that underlying layer of uncertainty about Brandon. I'd never seen him act like this before. Confident and direct was one thing, but aggressive and borderline hostile, to the people I knew he loved, was like he'd been replaced with his double from an alternate universe.

Did he have a goatee he was shaving off every morning to hide his evil self?

When Brandon got home, his mood was lighter and more playful. The sex was rough and fast—not that I was complaining—but the shift in attitude was disconcerting.

When the three of us went to bed, Brandon stayed. There was no creeping out of the room an hour later to go compose.

But I was intently aware that he spent most of the night tossing and turning.

22 /
danny

I 'd been to fantasy conventions before, and I'd been to professional events where vendors wooed high-end clients.

RinCon was a chaotic blend of both. When the doors to the convention center opened, gamers, cosplayers, and other fans swarmed in to get a glimpse of their favorite companies' latest and greatest. Outside this room, executives were making deals behind closed doors that would rock the gaming world a year from now, or two.

The entire event was its own unique form of creation through entropy, and I loved it.

The volume in the room grew several decibels within a matter of minutes. Some booths had a barker drawing people in, others had their demos playing for the world to hear, and of course, the chatter. Brandon could probably do an amazing mix with samples of these sounds.

The AcesPlayed booth already had a line of people waiting for a chance at the demo. We had more than our share of detractors as well—people stopping to sneer at the *disgusting* game content, before stepping to the Rinslet booth next to ours, to play a game that let them shoot anything that moved.

Everyone from AcesPlayed was here somewhere in the building, either in meetings, answering questions, or taking their turn at security.

I was working with Link. Our job was basically to keep the peace. With his broad shoulders, square jaw, and resting bitch face, he was exactly the kind of big, burly bear I would've hooked up in a heartbeat in those years between Reese and Brandon. He just had to look at someone with his brow furrowed, and they'd step back.

He was also one of the nicest guys on the Development team. "No shit. Seether?"

"True story. We managed to make the docket for Ozzfest when they played in Denver. Not as us. The Used needed last-minute guitar and drums, and we were available." I didn't mind sharing stories about Plaid Peanut Butter way back when, though this was one of Reese's favorites, and she told it much better than I did.

"My D string broke five minutes into the set, and it wasn't like we had any crew or backup. My choice would've been to step off stage and restring, and kill the entire performance. They stopped the music; my mind was racing and I was looking back at Reese for a sign. Bert's ad-libbing with the audience, and giving me questioning looks in between. Shaun walked out onto stage, waved to the crowds when they went nuts, and handed me his guitar. Told me *don't break this one*."

"You call them by their first names." Link grinned. "Like you know them."

"We were introduced. It'd be weird to say Mr. Morgan, wouldn't it? Especially after I had my hands all over the guy's instrument."

Link snorted a laugh. "I guess so."

"Hey." Chris stopped in front of us. "Dr. Jekyll is looking for you."

He must mean Brandon, and I assumed the nickname meant Brandon was in a good mood so far this morning, but I wasn't thrilled about hearing someone else call him that. "Who?"

Chris rolled his eyes. "Brandon. He's in the main ballroom. I'll take your place."

"Thanks." I headed off to find *Dr. Jekyll*.

He and Dustin were still tweaking the audio for the Aces presentation this afternoon, but they thought they finally had it fixed.

"Do me a favor, go sit in the middle of the room," Brandon said. "Make sure you can hear and understand Dustin, and then move someplace else."

Seemed simple enough. I spent the next hour or

so doing exactly that, while Dustin and Brandon tested and tweaked the sound system. When Dustin pronounced it *done*, Brandon looked pleased.

"You're the best. Thank you." Brandon gave me a quick kiss before we parted ways.

The rest of the day was bedlam. Because I hadn't been part of the original schedule, I found myself running from person to person, delivering messages, standing in, and fixing last minute issues that sprang up if the person responsible was busy with something else.

Dustin's presentation was a hit, and when he was done, the booth was busier than ever.

By the time Brandon and I got home, we were drained. We barely managed to strip out of our clothes before crashing in bed.

Tuesday was more of the same. Not that I minded. Most of the people at Aces were good company, and the work was the right kind of challenging. But at the end of the day, Brandon had traded in easy going for a non-stop scowl, and I was ready for tomorrow to get here and be gone.

On Wednesday, I was working security again, this time with Nigel, when a familiar voice said *boo* in my ear. I grinned and turned to face Reese. "You made it." I gave her a quick hug.

"Like I was going to miss this spectacle?" She pointed toward the back of the exhibitor hall. "There's a guy over there, ripped as fuck, wearing flesh-colored briefs and nothing else. Don't tell me he's one of your characters."

"He's probably a Titan," Nigel said. "Naked, but way more naked than you expected?"

Reese scrunched up her nose—so adorable—"I guess?"

"Titan." Nigel sounded certain.

I wasn't arguing with a guy who could juggle knives when he was drunk.

"What are the odds one or both of you can break away for lunch?" Reese asked.

"I'm good, thanks," Nigel said. "Oh. Wait. You didn't mean me."

I suppressed a chuckle. "You can join us if you want."

He shook his head. "I'm good, thanks," he repeated.

Reese looked at me expectantly.

"Maybe?" I shrugged. Things weren't as busy today as they had been, but that was the difference between a loud roar and a dull roar. "I might beg you to grab me something instead. And I have no idea where Brandon is."

She squeezed my fingers. "I'll text him. What do you want?"

"There's a pizza place out in the hall that looks good." I handed her some cash.

"Be back soon."

I wasn't surprised that *soon* was more than half

an hour, but I was happy to see Brandon with Reese when she returned. I got Jeremy to relieve me, and Reese, Brandon, and I ducked into a curtained section of the booth that we'd set aside specifically for employees to get away. The convention still roared immediately on the other side of the fabric, but at least we had a smidgen of privacy.

There wasn't a lot of talking while we stuffed our faces. My brain was too tired for conversation and Brandon's was probably the same.

When we finished, Reese asked, "Do you want me to stick around? Or will I be in the way?"

"You're never in the way." I did want her here, but I didn't imagine standing around watching us watch everyone else would be super fun.

"Do you think we have time for a quickie back here?" Brandon's question came out of nowhere.

I wasn't sure how to respond. The two of them may be exhibitionists, but our lack of walls were an ill-timed bump from us becoming a live version of the game, if the three of us got down and dirty behind the curtains.

"Brandon? Danny?" Judith's call saved me from answering Brandon's question.

Brandon huffed. "Back here."

Judith joined us, a man by her side. It was a tight fight in here with all five of us. Both of them screamed *executive* in their suits. What would the dude in barely any clothing think of them, and vice versa?

"Reese. I heard you were here, I'm glad." Judith gestured at the man with you. "This is Dominic Mancini. Best damn contract lawyer there is."

He extended his hand. "Pleasure to meet you. I understand you've got a bit of an issue."

Reese shook Dominic's hand. "I'm sure I've got a lot of issues."

"With a contract." Dominic chuckled. "The rest are between you and God."

Reese looked between him and Judith, then at us. "I appreciate the introduction, but I can't afford a shitty lawyer, let alone *the best*."

"This is a favor for Judith," Dominic says. "I assume she'll own your soul after, but I hear she's kind about that."

"I'm not buying any more souls. The ones I have are trouble enough." Judith glanced sideways at Brandon.

Or I imagined it.

"But I am hoping we can get you and the band in for some contract work, once you're free and clear," Judith said.

Reese worked her jaw. "So, this is for real?"

Dominic nodded. "I was going to give you a call later in the week, but we heard you were here and I figured it was better to meet in person."

They discussed some basics about what Reese

was dealing with, and agreed she'd send him a copy of her contract. I saw a tension drain away that was typically a normal part of being around Reese.

As he went to leave, I stopped him. "If her manager told her he'd let her out of the contract for sleeping with him, does that help her case at all?"

Dominic's good mood vanished behind anger. "I wish it did, but unlikely. What a scumbag."

"That's not fair to scum." Reese's laugh was tight.

"I need to run," Dominic said. "Email me everything, tell this asshole to contact me directly for anything going forward, and I'll be in touch in the next day or two."

Reese was bouncing when Dominic and Judith left. "I actually have hope. For the first time in ages. Wow."

"You deserve it." I gave her a long kiss. Her moan against my lips was delicious.

Brandon wrapped an arm around her waist, tugged her away, and crushed his mouth to hers. The sight was sexy as fuck to watch, but startling. Were we at that point? Were they? Apparently so. More hope sparked in my chest.

Reese hung around the rest of the day, an unofficial Aces team member, and helped us break everything down when the show was over.

As we were wrapping up, Judith grabbed my attention. "Real quick, and I'll let you get home. I want to extend your contract. Have you in the office a few days a week, and on call when you're okay with it and when Luna can't be."

"I… Yeah, okay." I hadn't expected to be doing Aces work much longer. Luna and I had put the finishing touches on what I was contracted to do, and everything else was clean-up.

"See. Easy peasy," Judith said. "I'll get you a more official notice tomorrow, but I wanted to check with you tonight."

I thanked her again, and she was on her way.

"We have to celebrate," Reese said.

Which sounded fun, but also I was exhausted from the last three days. "Does celebrating involve sitting on the couch doing nothing and eating takeout?"

"I don't see why not." Brandon already had his phone out. "What do we want? We'll pick something up on the way home, and then we don't have to go anywhere or do anything once we're inside."

We picked up Mexican, and headed home. The celebration was tame, and we cheered as much for Reese's good news as mine. It felt good to have the two of them here. All of us connected like this, cheering for each other's successes.

After dinner, the giddy mood turned to making out and sex. Fast. Hard. Frantic. With Brandon initiating.

We were spent when we collapsed in bed. I was

going to sleep like the dead tonight. I was right on that cusp of passing out, when the mattress shifted, and Brandon crept from the room.

And there went the ability to sleep.

"No, really, is it me?" Reese asked softly.

I cuddled her close, unable to hide my frustration. "No. It's not you, it's him."

And I didn't have any idea what to do about it.

23 /
brandon

I shouldn't have stayed up so late. I knew it was a mistake as I was climbing out of bed last night. Not just because I was already drained from RinCon, but Danny was hurt. There was no ignoring the look he gave me when he woke me up this morning.

The cool *hello-slash-goodbye* from Reese on her way out, wasn't great either.

I had to get the notes out of my head though. After so many days of being locked away from that part of my mind, I needed to make something that sounded beautiful.

I wasn't sure I'd succeeded, the results leaned more toward haunting, but they were a rough start of the song I heard in my head.

Danny would be in the office later today, but for this morning I was on my own. The way it had been for ages. Same old shit, different day. I couldn't muster the enthusiasm to do anything when I reached the Music room at work.

Fortunately, I wasn't the only one dragging after yesterday. Ivan was an angel, and had extra coffee waiting for all of us in the breakroom, along with bagels and donuts.

The sugar and carb crash would be brutal in a few hours, but it would happen now without the boost, so I indulged.

My morning meetings were low-key, thanks to everyone's post-con crash. I was looking forward to staring blankly at the wall for a little bit when Sonya and Jeremy knocked on my open door.

"Do you have a few minutes?" Sonya asked.

Not really. "Sure."

They grabbed a couple of chairs and wheeled up to my computer. "It's about the music you gave me for the new quest line," Sonya said.

Not my best work, but better than I'd done in a while. Composed after one of those incredible sex sessions with Danny and Reese. "Epic right?"

"Yes." Sonya's reply was enthusiastic.

"But also, no," Jeremy said.

I directed a glare at him, and he stared back.

Sonya ducked her head. "The thing is, I'm not sure the tone matches the story."

"Really? I didn't see anything about using a specific tone in the requirements." My retort came out with more of an edge than I intended.

"I tried to make it clear." Sonya was quiet.

Jeremy growled. "And I quote, *setting is light and joyous, with a hint of fun, and a lot of brightness.*"

"The game is half neon. Brightness is subjective." I couldn't ignore the defensiveness surging inside.

"No, I know," Sonya said. "And that's why we're talking now. Tell me what you need, in order to lighten up the music."

"Lighter, I got it." I bit off the words.

"Okay. Thanks." Sonya stood with a frown.

Jeremy smacked the desk. "No. Not okay. What the fuck crawled up your ass and died?"

I really wasn't in the mood to fight, and I had snapped. "I don't know. I didn't mean it."

"But you did, because you doubled down."

I clenched my jaw. "Fine. How about it always bugs me, and I'm tired of not saying so."

"Feedback always bugs you?" Jeremy scoffed. "Since when? I don't know what your problem is— your boyfriend isn't putting out, you've got sand in your shorts, whatever—but don't take it out on Sonya."

"Excuse me?" I didn't appreciate the personal attack.

"You heard me. If you're looking to pick a fight, I'm here, but leave Sonya out of it. And if you want to fling insults and whine and say *I'm unhappy*, I'll give as good as you."

I stared him down, tempted to say something I'd regret about two seconds after it left my mouth. Why couldn't that filter have kicked in five minutes ago? "I'll fix the music." My tone was neutral again. "Feedback is fine. I'll listen more objectively next time."

"Great. Thanks." Jeremy didn't sound like he meant it.

Which was fine, I wasn't sure I did either.

After they left, the encounter played on a loop in my mind. What was wrong with me? Seriously, what was I doing? And why couldn't I stop?

I didn't know, but I suspected if Jeremy walked back in here now, I'd try to pick a fight with him again. I scrubbed my face, and groaned into my fingers when my desk phone rang.

I grabbed it without looking. "Yeah."

"Go home Brandon," Judith said.

What? "Why?"

"Because I'm the boss and I said so. Go home. Stay there until next year."

Yep, there was the surge of irritation again. I swallowed back a retort, amid the scream in my mind asking *would it be so bad if she fired you?*

It would be. It really really would. "Fine. I'm gone." I hung up the phone, not caring that it clattered in the cradle.

24 /
danny

I t was both strange and felt right, being back here. Not because of the three days of RinCon —I'd attended with Brandon for years—but that I was a part of it, both the event and the workplace. I was no longer an observer, or *Brandon's boyfriend*. People greeted me like I belonged here as I walked through the building, and I felt like I did.

When I gave up this line of work, years ago, I never imagined myself coming back to it. But this environment was different. It was better.

"This is so much easier with a second set of eyes and a second brain," Luna said. "Ooh, do you think I could grow a second brain?"

I stared at her. "Would you want to? You'd think twice as much."

"That's kind of the point."

I shook my head. "About everything. Not just cybersecurity."

Luna wrinkled her nose. "Fine. I see your point. I'll just have to keep using yours then."

"I'm at your disposal."

We continued working. A short while later, one of my alerts pinged. I thought I'd cleared all of those out after we figured out the stolen assets problem.

Oh. This was related to the video posted of Reese and I, singing at the Christmas party. I had a match for the account it had come from. I clicked through the wall of text that was my code's digital brain-dump, sifting out important bits of information, following links, and noting names.

Realization spread through me when I finally reached a source account. I didn't recognize the woman in the photos, but I did recognize the man she said was her sister's husband. *Todd.* Reese's agent. I needed to tell her. Tell Brandon. Tell whoever this magical attorney was that Judith was supposedly hooking Reese up with.

"So, um… tell me to shut up if you don't want to talk about it." Luna's timid request yanked my attention from the information. "But, is Brandon okay?"

I shouldn't be surprised she noticed—Luna picked up a lot on people's emotions. "He's struggling a little, but he'll be fine." Hopefully that was vague-but-reassuring.

"Okay…"

That was the end of that.

"But, I mean—" Luna looked up from her work. "The thing today wasn't an isolated incident."

Thing today? "What thing?"

She worried her bottom lip. "With Sonya and Jeremy?"

I frowned and motioned for her to keep talking.

"And Judith told him to take the rest of the year off." Luna finished quietly. "I figured you'd know."

I figured I'd know, too. *Fuck.* Why didn't he tell me that? Call me when he was leaving. Something? "He's probably just cooling down or something." I was already texting him.

I heard something happened at work. You okay? I wrote.

It took too long for his reply to come through, and I couldn't focus on my work as minutes ticked away. I jumped when my phone finally chirped with an answer.

It's nothing. I'll see you tonight. Don't worry about it.

That was some of the least comforting language he could've used. Especially coming from Brandon, in the middle of the work day, when his boss had told him not to work.

Hell yes I was going to worry. "I need to cut out early." I felt bad doing so a whole day after they offered me a longer contract, but I wasn't going to get anything done staying here.

Luna nodded. "I understand. Let me know if I can help."

"Thanks." I didn't even know what I was going to do, let alone what I'd ask anyone else to do for us.

The drive home was torture, despite the afternoon traffic being light, and by the time I got inside, my anxiety was cranked to *maximum*.

Brandon was in the music room, but the door was open, and he wasn't moving. Instead, he was wearing his headphones and staring at the electric keyboard. He didn't look up when I walked in.

I touched his shoulder to get his attention, and he jumped.

His startled scowl turned to a smile when his gaze landed on me. "What are you doing home?" he asked.

"You had to know your reply wouldn't reassure me. I want your side of what happened at the office."

"That can wait." Brandon grabbed my wrist and pulled me between his legs. As he stood, he pressed his body to mine, and then his mouth to mine, as he gripped the back of my neck.

I pressed a palm to his chest and pushed him back enough to breathe. "It can't wait."

Brandon's expression went flat.

This wasn't right. None of it. "What's going on?"

"Same shit as always. I told you, I'm dealing with it."

I pulled his headphones off and set them aside, then looked him in the eye. "But you're not."

"I'm trying." Brandon turned away.

I didn't want to make accusations, but we'd said so much up to this point and not dug deep enough to say the right things. "Are you?"

"What are you trying to say?"

"Do you remember when we started dating?" I wouldn't have this memory so near the surface if I hadn't talked to Reese about it the other day. It was healing and soothing then. Now it cranked my anxiety higher. "When I started drinking again?"

"Yes."

I needed him to look at me. I grabbed his arm and spun him back to face me. "I won't watch you destroy yourself."

"This isn't the same at all." Brandon scoffed and shook his head.

"You're not an alcoholic, or dealing with a different chemical addiction, but you are on a self-destructive path. You're not acting like yourself. *Everyone* sees it. The fucking developers see it, and Chris has the empathy of a potato."

Brandon jerked away and brushed past me. "I told you, I'm coping." He walked out of the room.

"But you're not." I followed him up the stairs and into the living room. "Shoving your emotions into a box and saying *I'll power through* isn't coping."

He whirled on me, anger flashing in his eyes.

"I'm not in one of your group sessions. Don't treat me like a basket case."

I stared back in disbelief. Where was I supposed to go next? I wanted to snap at him and tell him not to imply those kids were crazy, and just as badly, I wanted to know why the fuck he was pissed off.

Brandon pinched the bridge of his nose. "I didn't mean it that way."

"There aren't a lot of ways to interpret what you said. How *did* you mean it?"

"I'm not saying you're— Just because you did that stuff— I know it helped—"

"Stop." I couldn't listen to him call therapy and AA *that stuff.* "You're making this worse."

Brandon turned away again, pacing with his hands jammed in his pockets. "I have a few weeks off, and I'll use it to regroup."

"That needs to include talking to me. Or Phillip. Or a professional. Or someone."

"We are talking."

I stepped in his path. "We're dancing around the issue and saying a whole lot of nothing, rather than getting into what's eating you alive."

"What do you want from me?" Brandon snapped.

"You. I want you. To confront the source of the mood shifts. I want you to be you again."

"This is who I am. I hit a rough patch and now you can't handle me?"

I clenched my jaw at the accusation and tried to temper my frustration. Screaming at Brandon wouldn't help, but talking to a brick wall wasn't working either. "I will walk through Hellfire with you. But I won't stand at the edge of the pit and watch you drown in it because you refuse to grab the rope."

"Because I've got it under control."

Cue the internal screaming. "Sitting back and telling yourself you'll do better is not *control*."

"It's the best I've got."

If we kept going, we'd also keep talking in circles. I couldn't do this. The realization ached like few things in my life had. The last time I hurt this much was when Reese left me, but this time…

This time I had to be the one to make that decision. *Damn it.* The shout echoed in my head. "Call me when that changes." I walked toward the door.

Brandon grabbed my arm, digging his fingers in. "Where are you going?"

"Reese's. I don't know beyond that." I jerked out of his grip.

"You've said, over and over, you'd never leave me for her."

Rage and impotence and grief bubbled inside, threatening to choke me. "I'm not. I'm leaving you for us."

"You're as bad as everyone else. Things get tough and you walk away. Fuck you."

I didn't answer. I couldn't. I grabbed my keys and walked out the door.

When I was halfway down the street, I let out the scream of frustration I'd been holding in, and kept shouting until my throat was raw. When I couldn't make any more sound, I hammered the sides of my fists on the steering wheel instead. Did I really just do that? I couldn't believe it. Were things that bad?

No, but they were getting there fast, and if this yanked Brandon back, the pain was worth it.

And if it didn't...

If it didn't, if he continued down the path he was on, then I'd made the right choice.

It took way too long, and not nearly long enough, to reach Reese's apartment. I knocked.

She answered, and frowned when her gaze met mine. "What happened?"

Of course it was written all over my face. Always. Why did I have to be the guy who wore my heart on my sleeve? "I left Brandon."

"Oh. Fuck me." Reese tugged me inside, closed the door, and wrapped her arms around me.

I squeezed back, holding onto her for all I was worth.

25 /
brandon

How dare he?

The thought roared through my head as I clenched and unclenched my fist.

"How *dare* he." Saying the words out loud sprinkled pepper on my anger, giving it a new taste. I couldn't think. Could see anything but red.

A blur of white caught the corner of my eye, and I whirled on the popcorn strung around the living room. "Not only did you leave, you went straight to her." I ripped a strand from the wall.

It was up there because of her. Was all of this her fault? "Reese." If a name had power, hers evoked envy. Ferocity. "I knew him letting you come back was a mistake. I *knew* it." I forced the words through clenched teeth. "He was fine. I was fine. *We* were good."

"And now this." I stalked into the music room. Her drums were the most obvious thing in here, against the back wall, taking up so much space, like baggage from his past.

I wanted her shit out of sight. Out of our home. One by one I dragged Reese's drums, and then her guitars, into the shed behind the house. I wasn't far gone enough to damage them, but *fuck* the temptation was there.

How could Danny do this? "You know things take work. You know how much pain she's capable of causing. You *know* how much it hurts to have your heart ripped out. And you gave up on us."

The music room looked empty now, but Reese's perfume and Danny's cologne still permeated the air in here. Danny's guitars mocked me from their various resting spots. I couldn't look at this. I stormed out of the room and slammed the door shut behind me.

"At least you weren't a complete idiot about surrendering." I didn't care that I was talking to the air. If Danny wasn't here to listen, I'd say it anyway. I'd talk to myself. "At least you weren't stupid about it like Dad was." I almost choked on the words and the pain attached to them. "Am I really the only person I know who can see things through?"

Why did the world have to feel so heavy, like a weight pressing in on my chest?

Why was I so cold to Adam? Why did I push Danny away?

The questions came out of nowhere, blindsiding

me and knocking my thoughts off balance. Frustration and grief bled in to taint the rage.

"Why did I give up on such a good thing, Danny?" I asked the empty room. "Why couldn't I admit that Reese—"

Why did Danny have to leave the way he did? Why wasn't I good enough to point out why he should stay? What did I do wrong?

I sank to my knees in the middle of the living room, tears streaming down my face.

26 /
reese

I never thought I'd be here again. Danny in my bed. Us with a solid relationship.

I also never would've guessed it would be under these circumstances. We sat facing each other, legs crossed, knees touching. His grief was palpable. I wanted to wrap him up and chase it all away. I knew what he was feeling, because it was how I felt when I pushed him out of my life. Which also meant if Brandon had any shred of humanity—which he did —he was feeling the same thing right now.

But my focus was Danny.

"Do you want to talk about it?" We'd been sitting in silence for long enough I'd lost track of time. I wasn't sure what to say beyond offering sympathy and hugs, and we'd moved past that. I hoped he'd open up on his own, but he needed a nudge.

He shook his head. "Not really. No."

"Okay."

"I mean, I wanted to talk to Brandon," Danny said. "That was all I wanted. For him to tell me something with more substance than *I've got this*. Should've been a simple request, right?" He looked at me. "Am I the unreasonable one?"

"No." Even without details, I knew Danny had tried, and I was filling in blanks here and there with the snippets he fed me.

He tossed his keys, wallet, and phone on the comforter next to us. "This is all I walked out with. I'm going to have to go back and get my stuff—" His voice cracked.

"Not tonight. We'll deal with that step if it gets here."

"He hasn't called." Danny toggled the screen on and off on his phone. "No text. He didn't try to stop me."

"Would that have been better?" I didn't know which direction to push him. I couldn't blame Danny, but I also couldn't imagine him without Brandon. All I could do was try to get a grasp on what he wanted.

I doubted he had any more idea than I did.

"No," Danny said. "Maybe. I might have stayed, and it feels like that enables him. But I don't know. I made the right decision, didn't I?"

"You did what you needed to do at the time."

Danny looked at me, wrinkles of disbelief marring his forehead. "That's not an answer, Reese. It's a *yes* or *no* question."

"If I tell you *no*, you didn't make the right decision, you'll continue to question yourself regardless. If I tell you *yes*, a teeny part of you will ask why I want to see the two of you apart. You may not even realize it, though in your case you'll probably just hate yourself for it." When I wasn't trying to guess —project my own feelings—how he felt about me, I had a pretty good idea how Danny's mind worked.

He sighed. "Judith told him to take the rest of the year off, because he was pissing off everyone he talked to in the office. That's how bad it is. And I can't... I don't... That's not Brandon."

"Everyone struggles sometimes. You're perfect, and even you had a rock bottom moment."

Danny almost smiled. "I'm not perfect."

"Agree to disagree."

He grasped my fingers and kissed the back of my knuckles. "Thank you."

"I didn't do anything."

"For being you. For being Reese. For being my wonderful and amazing best friend."

Best friend. Tonight was not the time to pick that apart. "Always."

My full-size mattress was too small for two people, but that didn't stop Danny and me from curling up with each other and staying that way the entire night. Waking up next to him was incredible. Right. I didn't see it ever getting old.

But the warm glow his presence left inside was muted by his reasons for being here.

He nuzzled my neck and I rolled over to face him.

"What's on the docket for today?" I asked.

"Work. I need the distraction while I process. I need clothes, too." Danny frowned. "I guess… a stop by my friendly neighborhood twenty-four-hour store, for something super Casual Friday." He was making decisions without questioning them.

That seemed like a good sign, even if none of them had to do with Brandon. I kissed the tip of Danny's nose. "Go shower. I'll make you coffee, and I'll be here when you're done for the day."

Danny's smile was sad and so unlike him. "Yes, ma'am." He was a few steps across the room when he paused. "*Fuck*, I almost forgot."

"That doesn't sound good." I wasn't sure I could handle any more surprises now.

He looked at me. "I think it might be. Good, that is. Did you know Todd is married? Or at least, someone thinks they're married to him."

"Uh, no." Not that I gave a shit about his

personal life, and why wasn't I surprised that the sleazeball trying to coerce me into sex had someone at home. Poor woman. "That's good news?"

Danny huffed out a tight laugh. "Her sister works at the hotel where we had the Christmas party. She—the sister—posted the video of us that went viral."

It was early and my brain hadn't switched all the way on, but the pieces came together in my mind to form a picture that both made sense and didn't, and was infuriating. "Do you think Todd had her post it?"

"It seems like something he'd do, doesn't it? Especially now that you know why he's held this contract over you?"

Fuck me. He was married. He was even sleezier than I thought, and that was both impressive and disgusting. "I assume you have links? Proof?"

"I do."

"Get ready for work. I'm sending this to Dominic."

I didn't expect to hear back until later in the day —a guy like that had to be busy, and probably had an assistant screening his messages—so I was surprised when a reply came through before Danny emerged from the shower.

This is beautiful. Send me the links when you have a moment. This will make everything easier. I'll get back to you with more by Monday.

Talk about conflicted. This was the most hope I'd had in years about getting out of my contract, but the mood was tempered by my concern for Danny.

And Brandon. I hoped he was okay.

I sent Danny on his way with a kiss, which was so odd but so right. The thought about Brandon wouldn't leave.

Going to see him was probably a bad idea, but it wasn't like he'd take my calls. And who knew? Maybe I'd piss him off enough for him to stop being a dick and go after who he needed.

I made myself wait, to give me time to talk myself out of the stupid idea, but by ten, I couldn't think of anything else. When I got to Brandon and Danny's—I had to still call it that, or I was giving up —Brandon's car was in the driveway.

I knocked and waited.

He opened the door, rolled his eyes, and flung it shut again as he turned away.

This wasn't going down like that. I wedged my foot into place, and stepped into the house behind him.

"You're literally the last person I want to see right now." Brandon walked into the living room, never looking back.

I followed him. "So don't look at me while I talk."

He stopped in the middle of the room, his back

to me. "What do you want, Reese? If you're here to gloat, fuck off."

"I'm not." Did he really think that little of me? I was going to bet on *he's being pissy, don't take it personally*. "I'm here because this isn't right. Because you're about to fuck up like I did. Don't do that."

"In case you heard a different story, I wasn't the one who left."

I wouldn't argue semantics with Brandon. "Adam told me what happened to your dad." Why did I say that?

Brandon faced me with a scowl. "Now I think you're just trying to make things worse."

"Maybe. I'm not good at this *giving advice* stuff."

"No shit. If the next thing you say is comparing your loss to mine, the two aren't even in the same country. Your mother didn't want to leave. My dad couldn't find a reason to stay."

"But Danny wants to find one. Just one." I really was bad at this.

Brandon clenched his jaw. "He has one. I love him, he loves me. How is that not a reason?"

"Do you think your dad didn't love you?"

"Don't try to psychoanalyze me. You suck at it."

"Fine." I let out a growl of frustration both at me and him. "How about I be blunt, then? I don't want to see you broken up, and it's only partly because it kills me to see Danny hurting. The two of you are amazing together. Pull your head out of your ass, consider what he's asking of you, and decide if your stubbornness is worth the cost of losing him."

"Get the fuck out. *Now*."

27 /
danny

I was numb. I had to be. It was the only way to make it through Friday. Through Reese's sympathy. Through being conscious.

When Adam called me on Saturday, I almost didn't answer. Not because of him, but he made me think of Brandon and if I did that for too long, this carefully crafted bubble of Novocain would crumble.

This wasn't his fault in any way. "Hello?" I answered.

"Hey. Um… how are you?"

"I've been better. What's up?"

"What's wrong?" Adam asked.

Telling Reese was hard. Adam was a good guy, but he wasn't a *let me air my dirty laundry with you* kind of friend. If he was asking, he didn't know what happened between Brandon and I, which meant he probably still wasn't speaking with his brother either.

"Some stuff." *I'm coping.* The words nearly choked me.

"I need a favor, please. I hate to ask, I know you've done so much, but I don't dare ask Brandon —I don't care if you tell him, just don't get him involved—and I don't want my friends to see me if I flip out and—"

"What's up?" I was not only curious, but helping Adam meant I didn't have to think about my own problems.

He sighed. "Richard called me. From jail. He wants me to visit. He wants to talk to me."

Oh. "Wow."

"Yeah. I don't know what to think, but I need to confront him. I was hoping you'd go with me. Moral support or some shit."

Sounded like a weird outing, but it was a distraction. Adam let me pick the time, and it made the most sense for me to go while Reese was working. She didn't need me staring at her and moping while she was talking to clients.

I met Adam in the parking lot. This entire place was intimidating, which was another distraction from the bleakness that had moved into my heart. Inside, we were processed and shown to a waiting room. A moment later, Richard was shown in from another door. He took a seat across from us.

He and Adam stared at each other as seconds ticked away.

"I'm sure you have a lot of questions," Richard finally said.

"Just one. Why?"

Richard dropped his head so his chin rested against his chest. "I made a few bad business deals. More than a few. Before I met you. What you're doing really is incredible, I was honest about that. But I'm in so far over my head... I'm drowning and I couldn't find my way to the surface."

I couldn't imagine that being in here helped, especially with the charges he'd face for opening fire on the police, but I kept my mouth shut.

"I panicked when I saw the bills stacking up, and that insurance money on the workshop was so tempting," Richard said. "I thought I had it figured out. That I knew exactly how to start the fire so they wouldn't know it was me."

Adam stared at him, eyes wide. "Fucking hell, dude. I lost so much work. I could've been killed. I... I can't even."

"I know. I'm sorry."

"What about the game demo you stole from us?" I didn't mean to speak up, but we were here and he was confessing.

Richard looked at me as if he'd forgotten I was here. "You figured that out. I didn't mean to."

"You obviously did." Adam picked up on my cues despite me not having told him the details. I'd owe him that information later. "Something like that doesn't happen by accident."

"I just, I saw the assets on the network, and games get funded all the time that never get made. It should've been easy money. No one was supposed to get hurt."

"You stole someone else's work." Adam scoffed. "You set fire to my apartment. You shot at the police. What the fuck?"

"I wanted them to shoot back." Richard's voice was quiet.

"Fucking coward." Adam stalked up to the door and pounded until they let us out.

I followed Adam outside, sifting through any appropriate response. I was dating Brandon when their father took his life. I knew how hard it hit both brothers.

"Why do people think that's an answer? I don't understand." Adam was talking more to himself than to me, and he was more concerned about the shootout than the money.

I wasn't surprised, and I didn't have an answer he wanted to hear.

"I get it." Adam kept talking and walking without input from me. "There's not always a way out of a bad situation, besides to go through it. But he let himself fall that far…" He stopped at his car, hands on the hood and face dropped between his arms as he dragged in shuddering breaths.

The only thing I could do was give him the truth. I'd never reached the point where I decided to end it all, but there was more than one night where I wished I could drink enough I never woke up. The memory rushed back raw, like an old wound being sliced open again, reminding me how much I didn't want to lose Brandon.

"Sometimes it's hard to see how far you've fallen until you hit rock bottom. And once you're there, it's hard to climb out. There's no will left. No strength." God I hoped I'd done the right thing with Brandon.

"I can't... Just no." He wouldn't look at me. "Thank you for coming with me."

"Any time. Will you be all right?"

Adam shook his head. "I'm going to be pissed off for a long time. If that's okay, then sure, why the fuck not."

I didn't have a comeback.

28 /
reese

I didn't like seeing Danny mope, but I didn't know what else to do. Focusing on the fact he was here, with me, helped. I still hated seeing him so sad, though.

After he got back from the jail with Adam, his mood was even more somber. Through the rest of Saturday and most of Sunday, he said very little.

Sunday night, Dominic called, to see if I was available for a face to face with Todd on Monday.

The thought of seeing Todd again churned my gut. "I might not be able to resist punching him in the throat."

"I'll make sure to keep the two of you separated, then." Dominic chuckled. "When the conversation is over, if you still want to clothesline him, I'll look the other way so there are no witnesses."

"I'm going to hold you to that."

Monday, I sent Danny off to work, dressed in

my most professional attire, and headed to the address on Dominic's business card. The firm had his name on it, which was impressive by itself. What little I knew about lawyers told me if the guy at the top was willing to carve out time for me, I should feel special.

Their offices were downtown, only about six blocks from AcesPlayed. Close enough to visit Danny when I was done, but far enough that this was an older part of town. The buildings here were a mix of classic architecture and new high rises.

And the law firm was in one of the restored older three-story buildings. The sleek metal and glass lobby with leather furniture screamed *money*. If I were paying for this, it wouldn't be cheap.

I gave the receptionist my name, and expected her to ask me to have a seat. I'd be waiting a while.

Instead, I was immediately shown to a small conference room. "Dom will be with you soon," The young woman told me.

Dom? I wasn't sure how I felt about that. "Thank you."

He walked into the room just a few minutes later, and took a seat next to me. "Sorry to make you wait."

"You really didn't." I tempered politeness with my anxiousness and the urge to get this over with. If I was going to hear *there's nothing I can do* I'd rather know it up front.

"Todd and his attorney are in another room already," Dominic said. "I asked them to arrive a little earlier. Figured it wouldn't hurt to make them wait."

I smirked. "I've always wondered if people do that."

"Normally I wouldn't, but this guy's sleazy with a capital Z. If I'd found your case, even without Judith's prompting, I'd have taken it. And I can't tell him this, because it might be interpreted as a threat, but I'm looking for every contract he has with bands. A lot of his deals are about to be broken, because there's no way you're the only one."

"You'll get no complaints from me." Was that hope blossoming inside? It was kind of hot.

He smiled. "When I get them in here, answer any questions I ask, but not any of theirs. Only talk to me."

Nothing else I'd tried so far had worked, and this sounded simple. "I'm not sure how much worse it could be so I put my musical career in your hands."

"I promise you'll love this." He picked up the phone in the middle of the table and told the person on the other end to show in Todd Grude and his lawyer.

As they sat down, Todd looked at me and opened his mouth.

"We have a counter offer to your lawsuit, and we'd like to settle today." Dominic talked over him.

I really liked this guy.

Todd snorted. "I'm listening."

"Good. Make sure you do," Dominic said. "The offer is, you let Ms. Ellis out of her contract, pay her any fees owed for the last five years—we'll arrange for the audit—and erase, delete, or otherwise destroy any copies you have of her work. You'll revert any and all rights you have to her recordings, songs, and anything else you currently control associated with Ms. Ellis."

"No." Todd laughed out the word.

Because really, what else was he going to say? Did Dominic think that would work?

He looked unfazed. "We have irrefutable evidence that you were associated with the posting of the video you're suing her for, which means she's not in breach of her contract."

Todd worked his jaw.

His lawyer shot him a look.

"N— No you don't," Todd stammered. "Because I wasn't. Why would you think that?"

"A case can and will be made for revisiting Ms. Ellis's contract. We'll present that it's out of date, intentionally vague, and needs to be updated for a modern era," Dominic said. "If you wish to pursue this part of the case, Mr. Grude, you may. You'll be responsible for your legal fees and court fees, as is standard in cases like this. You can listen to me explain to a judge—a jury if you decide to pursue things to that extent—that the only reason you're doing this is because you didn't get your dick wet fifteen years ago."

"Excuse me?" Todd's lawyer finally spoke up.

"You can't prove that, either," Todd said.

Dominic silenced both of them with a look.

I hoped whoever he was fucking appreciated how hot he was.

"Can you afford to fight me when I try?" Dominic asked. "Ms. Ellis can. I will dedicate an entire team to ensuring you're tied up in court for at least as long as you've consumed this talented woman's career. I doubt it will cost what she could have made, but it will be expensive."

Todd's furious look was priceless. Merry Christmas to me.

His lawyer looked at Dominic and then Todd, completely ignoring me. "You still owe me for the work I've already done. I have to advise you now, to take this offer."

"Don't fucking say that in front of them," Todd barked.

His lawyer shrugged. "It's true. That's my legal advice. Sign the paperwork and walk away. Or find another lawyer."

I was almost turned on right now. It was a good thing Danny's office wasn't far.

"Fine. I'll have someone else look over the offer and sign." Todd spoke through clenched teeth.

Dominic slid him a single sheet of paper. "This says that you'll do exactly what you just agreed to, and that as long as there is nothing in the settlement that we haven't discussed, you'll sign. I assure you, there's not."

Todd gripped the pen so hard it cracked as he signed the paper, and he stormed out of the office.

His lawyer gave us a short nod and followed.

"Oh my goddess, thank you so much." I let my gratitude tumble out the instant we were alone again. "Seriously. Thank you, thank you. I don't know what else I can do."

Dominic shook my hand. "Go. Sing. Use the second chance. And let me remind you Judith would like a bit of your time, on behalf of AcesPlayed, now that you're a free agent."

"What did she offer you in return?" Maybe it was rude to ask, but I had to know.

He shook his head. "A favor for my husband. That's all."

Did she always deal in favors? That sounded like a dangerous deal to make, and made me glad I'd made my arrangement with her up front. "Thank you again."

I could've walked to the Aces offices and it wouldn't have taken any longer, but I wanted to crank the stereo and sing along at the top of my lungs. I felt like a million bucks, and I was going to go surprise Danny and Brandon with the news.

No. Just Danny.

The mental slip made me stall. I wouldn't let it ruin the rest of the day, but it did put a damper on things.

I found Danny in the office he was sharing with Luna.

"How'd it go?" he asked.

I couldn't drag this out even for a heartbeat. I had to share. "I'm out of the contract. It's over."

"Oh my God, yay!" Luna clapped and reached for her phone.

Danny wrapped me in a tight hug, and a long kiss, and I was happy to return both.

I was vaguely aware of Luna repeating the news to someone, and I heard the shout both over the phone and down the hall. That would be Adrienne.

"So I can post videos of you singing online now?" Luna asked.

I didn't let go of Danny, but I maneuvered so I could see her. "Why do you have videos of me singing?"

"Because you guys wail in concert, and why wouldn't I get that on my phone?"

"You have to wait until the ink is dry and the rights reversion is official," I said. "But otherwise, yes."

"So happy for you." Adrienne came from behind, almost knocking me over with a hug.

I couldn't stop grinning. We celebrated for a while longer, and I walked down the hall to Judith's office.

She looked up, impassive expression in place. "I assume you're responsible for turning my office into a zoo?"

"Today I am." And I didn't even feel bad about it. "Thank you for introducing me to Dominic. I'm not selling my soul again, but my music is yours on a contract basis."

Judith cracked a smile. "I'm glad to hear that. I'll be in touch."

I turned away.

"Reese." A hitch in Judith's voice stopped me, and I looked at her again. "I realize it's not appropriate to ask, but you seem most likely to have and give me an answer. Is Brandon okay?"

Some of my mood faltered.

"That good, huh?" she asked.

I shook my head. "Give him a little more time? I get that you're running a business and you don't have a lot of time, but just a little longer."

"I don't wait on things for most people, but he really is a friend, despite the way our working relationship has changed," she said. "If you talk to him before I do, tell him I said Merry Christmas."

I doubted I would, but I agreed anyway.

A group of us went to lunch to celebrate, and mostly managed to ignore the empty spot where Brandon would normally be. At the end of the meal, I gave Danny a goodbye kiss and told him I'd see him at home.

Back at my apartment, I put on my headphones and danced and sang around the room. This felt good. Ridiculously good. Like a giant weight had been lifted from my chest.

Danny brought takeout home, and we celebrated some more with alcohol free bubbly grape juice and curry from my favorite place.

When we were done, we cleaned up and settled onto the bed to sit and watch TV.

The way Danny was watching me made me nervous. He'd barely smiled in days and now there was a spark of light in his eyes as he searched my eyes.

"Do I have something on my face?" I tried to keep my tone light.

He booped my nose. "This."

What the…? I laughed.

"I want to tell you something, but I don't want you to think I'm saying it because of Brandon." It was the first time Danny had said his name since that first night he showed up here.

And I was more on edge than ever. "Okay?"

"This is between you and me. The timing isn't good now, but there will always be an excuse and it's important I tell you now. This is because of you, and not because of my broken heart."

My emotions hovered on a ledge that divided hope and despair. "You're killing me, Smalls."

Danny smiled and cradled my cheeks in his hands. "I love you, Reese. I always have. It's been different kinds of love over the years, but I have always, always loved you. I see you now and my heart swells and I can't stop watching you and I love waking up next to you and..." He shook his head. "This is all cluttered."

"No. It's wonderful." I was laughing and crying at the same time. "It's amazing. It's... I love you too." It was hard to talk through the tears, so I crushed my mouth to his instead. "I love you so much, and I'm so sorry—"

He cut me off with another kiss. "I know you are. We wouldn't be here if I didn't believe it. You're such an important part of my world, Reese. I need you in my life. I want you by my side."

"I want to be here." It felt as important to say that as *I love you*. "I want to be here with you and never leave."

"I mean, not *never*," Danny teased. "You can't follow me to work every day. And you'd go nuts if I watched you work all the time."

When I laughed I nearly choked on my tears. "You're such a dork."

"I'm your dork though." He wiped a sleeve

across my cheek, smearing the tears more than drying them. He pressed his lips to mine.

"You are. And that means more to me than I could ever put into words."

A whisper in the back of my mind reminded me we weren't healed until he made things right with Brandon, but tonight was about Danny and me. We could conquer the world if we were together, and that included figuring out what to do about his stubborn ass of a boyfriend.

29 /
brandon

I spent my weekend fluctuating between rage and grief and resisting the urge to send Danny a text. I'd type messages then delete them.

Come back. Please.

I'll talk. I'm sorry.

Fine. Fuck you.

How did everyone convince themselves it was so easy to walk away from a situation? My dad. My brother. Danny.

Why didn't they understand how important it was to stick it out?

What if I left?

The sentence made my gut revolt and an acrid taste surged in my throat. Such a simple question that carried a nauseating meaning.

But I wasn't considering leaving this world behind—I still wanted to be here, and not because of spite. I liked it here. Checking out on life wasn't a consideration.

There were things I wanted to put behind me, though. Would it be such a big deal if I set aside what wasn't working?

I didn't quit. That wasn't who I was. If it wasn't working, I'd fix it.

Fuck, I missed Danny. Reese. Adam. Loathing raged inside that I'd fought with each of them. Why didn't they understand my side of things?

Those were the thoughts that haunted me until Phillip rang the bell on Monday night. When I answered the door, he said, "I thought you could use a friend."

"I'm not in the mood for company." Not if I had to explain myself to yet another person.

"Turns out I was right." Phillip shouldered me out of the way—what was up with people barging into my house—and strode into the kitchen to set down a pizza box and a six pack of Dew.

His actions were irritating, but they also tugged on memories of the past. The early days of working together. How much fun work used to be.

I didn't want to lose myself in the past in any way. "Now's really not a good time."

Phillip glanced past me to the living room, where tattered popcorn strands still littered the carpet, then he looked at the kitchen sink, which held a few days' worth of dishes. "Now's the perfect time."

"What do you want?" I was trying not to be abrasive. Not with him.

He toed out a chair, but didn't sit. "To talk."

Please God, no. "I don't want to talk."

"Fine. I'll talk, you listen."

"I don't want a lecture, either."

"No lecture." Phillip shook his head. "You and Danny split."

Fucking hell. "Is he telling the whole office?"

"He's not telling anyone, but I've never seen him smile less, and a guy puts the pieces together."

"But this isn't a lecture," I said flatly.

"Nope. I need to unburden my soul, and I need a friend."

And I couldn't turn him away. Not with a request like that. Plus, I didn't want to be alone with my thoughts. I gestured to the seats. "I'm listening."

Phillip grabbed plates and napkins from the cupboards, moving around my kitchen as comfortably as if it were his own. Because we'd been friends for so long, we'd spent that kind of time at each other's places.

When did I stop loving spending time with the people I came up with in this industry? No, that wasn't right. I still enjoyed his company—everyone else's—it was the work that was wearing me down. Why?

If I examined that thought, I'd start to consider why things fell apart with Danny, and I wanted to stay mad at him.

Phillip made himself comfortable at the table, grabbed a slice of pizza, and slid me the box.

The food smelled good—I hadn't eaten much in the last few days—but I had a mood to hold onto. "You wanted to talk?"

He popped the top on a soda, and washed down a bite of food. "You remember the accident?" Some of his cheer faltered in that question.

I didn't have to ask *which one*. When Phillip lost his wife and child, more than a decade ago, it devastated him. It wasn't too long after I'd lost my father. Neither of us had ever shared the details; back then we were too tough for things like *feelings*, and as time passed it was less appropriate to bring the topic up at random.

Not that I wanted to talk about losing my dad. Not even now. Not with anyone.

"I spent a lot of time alternating between blaming myself and asking myself what I could've done to save them." His cheer was completely gone.

And his words were a punch in the gut.

"I still do, but I deal with it better. Though, there was a point where I figured if I didn't let anyone get that close again, I'd be safe from that kind of pain," Phillip said.

"I'm sorry to hear that." Good story, but I

hadn't pushed Danny away, he left. I wanted Danny back. Fuck, this hurt.

"When I finally admitted it, I realized what I'd almost lost this time around."

I didn't know how to respond, but I didn't like being dumped on while I was dealing with a fresher broken heart than he was. He had his second chance at happily ever after. I'd just lost my first, and the only one I wanted.

I shoved a bite of pizza in my mouth so I didn't have to say anything, but Phillip's words nagged me and mingled with what Reese said when she visited.

Would it be such a bad thing if I quit?

Not life. Never. But…

Work?

"Why did you decide to stay? At Aces?" I asked.

Phillip had hired Adrienne to take his place because he'd planned to leave the company. "I realized what I was looking for was still there."

I didn't want to hear a sappy story about *true love*. "Adrienne and Dustin?"

Phillip's smile didn't push aside his lingering look of sadness. "No. Once I pulled my head out of my ass, I would've ended up with them anyway. For me, I need to be in a place where I can help people learn and grow."

"Of course." I didn't begrudge Phillip the desire, but that wasn't me. His words rolled around in my thoughts, along with the biggest ball of confusion in Salt Lake City. What was it I needed? What was missing?

Phillip pushed back from the table. "Keep the rest of the food. Adrienne and Dustin are freaks and don't like pineapple on their pizza." He pulled a business card from his wallet and set it on top of the box. "And call me. For any reason. I don't care if it's three in the morning and you just need someone to hear you scream incoherently."

I didn't know what to make of his statement or the card. I already had his number.

Phillip left, but I stayed at the table, staring at nothing and trying to both ignore and make sense of what he'd said and every thought and feeling those words tangled themselves with.

I grabbed the business card. *Marcie Weller, Licensed Clinical Social Worker* followed by contact information. On the back of the card, written in Phillip's familiar handwriting was *She works wonders. Call someone.*

Did calling her mean I couldn't fix this myself?

Did ignoring the offer mean I wouldn't get Danny back?

Or Reese?

That Adam wouldn't speak to me again—that the people at Aces wouldn't—and I'd lose the last family I had?

What was I supposed to do?

30 /
danny

Yesterday, last night, was a bright spot in the middle of pitch blackness. Was there such a thing as a light in the middle of the tunnel? I was so happy to have Reese back. Not just in my life, but more. My heart swelled every time I thought about it.

And then deflated when I remembered Brandon.

Reese woke me up with kisses. When she said *we need to talk* that bright spot dimmed. "Don't do that to a guy. Especially not right now."

"It's not like that." She pulled me into a sitting position on the bed.

I settled with my back to the wall and she curled up next to me. "What's it like, then?"

"I love you dearly, and you can stay in this little space for as long as you want. We can. But there are decisions you have to make. Things you need to resolve. You don't have to do it now, but you can't ignore that they exist."

I sighed. "I know." I hadn't heard from Brandon and I hadn't tried to contact him. I didn't want to leave him for good, but I couldn't ignore the possibility. "I'm not. Leaving him for good," I added, since she couldn't read my mind. "God, I hope not. I don't want to have to."

"I know."

The absurdity of us tossing *I know* back and forth at each other made me chuckle. "If he came back now and said he was sorry, I'd probably drop everything to go back to him. But *sorry* isn't enough."

"Because the two of you have tried that route," Reese said.

"And it was just words. Words that didn't go anywhere. How am I going to recognize the difference between him meaning what he says and me just wanting really badly for that to be the case?"

"I think you'll know."

"You have a lot more faith in me than I do."

Reese leaned more weight into me. "You're not the first person to say that to me."

"Where does your confidence come from?" Why couldn't I grasp some of the same?

"Me being amazing."

I let out another strained laugh. She really was incredible. "I meant about me."

"You're amazing too."

I shook my head in disbelief. She was a light in the darkness. So much had changed over the years. "You know what I mean."

"I know."

I stuck my tongue out at her.

"Look at us," Reese said. "We both made some *bad* decisions back in the day. Yes, I started it, and I own that, but we were both idiots."

She meant the break-up. The drinking. The contract.

"And I'm still paying for it," Reese said. "I accept that, but even after everything, we found our way back to each other. The way we were always meant to be."

I loved the sentiment, but, "What does that have to do with Brandon?"

"Because you and I aren't the only ones meant to be. He'll figure it out, and when he does, you'll recognize it. And in time—a year or ten—the two of you will be sitting across from each other, remembering how he almost fucked things up, and how you're both glad things got fixed."

"It's a pretty picture."

She nudged me playfully with her shoulder. "You're not the only one who can create an image with words. Tell me you can't visualize it."

I could, but I wished I couldn't. If it didn't happen, I'd hurt that much more, but I wanted to embrace the possibility. "Would you be okay with me being with him?"

"I mean, yeah. It's not like you're leaving me." Her confidence really was sexy. "And when he's not being an asshole, the two of you are incredible together."

"What about you and him?"

"When he's not being stubborn and I'm not being stubborn, he and I are good together too."

I really liked her confidence. "So you see yourself in that picture you created."

"Duh."

None of this offered answers, but it made me feel better regardless. "He has so much to make up for, even though it was such a short amount of time." That wasn't quite right. "It's actually not a big list, but it feels like the proof that he means it will need to be overwhelming."

Reese tilted her head up and kissed me on the forehead, before leaning into me again. "I know."

31 /
brandon

I couldn't get Phillip's visit out of my head. The memories and emotions the brief exchange summoned were more potent than the words themselves. Combined with what Reese said to me, everything glommed together to gnaw at the Danny-sized pit in my heart. I was pretty sure the hole was so big now, it would take two people to fill it.

I carried the business card with me all night. Fell asleep with it on the nightstand, and woke up to it taunting me.

If talking to this Marcie woman would help me get Danny back, I'd do it. A little after nine, I dialed her number, expecting to leave a message and not hear back until after the holidays.

The ache in my chest grew at the thought of not having Danny here for Christmas.

"Sunshine Grove Counseling, this is Marcie

Weller. May I help you?" Her voice was pleasant and even, like live ASMR.

I stalled, my rehearsed message no longer appropriate. "Hi, Ms. Weller. A friend recommended you. I'd like to make an appointment."

"It's Marcie, please. Is this for you? And your name?"

"Yes. It's Brandon." Who was I that I'd forgotten how to have a conversation? It was ridiculous that this basic exchange scared me.

"Brandon. Hi. What am I seeing you about?"

"Therapy? That's what you do, right?"

Her laugh was soft enough I barely heard it. "Yes. That's what I do. I have an opening this afternoon. Would you like to come in then?"

So soon? "I expected you to be booked this week." I wasn't ready to talk yet, or at all, but I couldn't ignore the spark of hope at being able to tell Danny... Reese... When did she become such an intricate part of the equation?

"I get a lot of cancellations the week of Christmas. What do you think?"

"Sure. This afternoon sounds great." I forced the words out before I could over-think them. I was so tired of thinking.

"Great. I'll see you then."

Making the appointment didn't soothe my fractured thoughts, but it added a new verse to the remix. Now I had a whole new tune of confusion to sing along to, and I could fidget instead of staring blankly at walls.

By the time I got to the office, I was struggling to sit still. There was no one else in the waiting room. The sound of chirping birds played over the loud-speaker, and the furnishings were all shades of gray and tan. Dull, but strangely soothing.

I'd only been waiting a few minutes when a woman who was probably about my age stepped out of one of the doors. "Brandon? Come on in."

Her office was a lot like the waiting room, but the desk and shelves behind it held a more personal touch. Books. Knickknacks. Etcetera.

There was a couch and a few chairs. "Do I lay down?"

"Not unless you want to. Pick a seat."

The couch looked good, so I settled in.

"You were a little vague on the phone. What did you want to see me about?" Marcie asked.

"I'm here so my friends will leave me alone and I can get my boyfriend back." Was the bluntness to shock her? To get me off the hook? Both probably.

She nodded. "Okay."

Not the reaction I expected.

"Tell me about your boyfriend. What's his name?" she said.

"His name is Danny." I could keep this vague. Like a list of statistics. Except, once I started talking, she didn't interrupt. She'd nod occasionally, or say *okay*, but nothing else. And the words fell out of my mouth without permission.

Not in any sort of order. It was a jumble of tangents that jumped from Danny to Reese to Adam. My dad. Work. I lost track of what I said, and I had no idea if it made sense.

"What do you remember about your dad?" The fact that her question was longer than a few syllables caught me off-guard.

I grasped the first thing that popped into my head. "When I was eight, I wanted a train set. Not just a set of tracks, but the full thing, with an intricate setup. We couldn't afford it. Adam was a baby and we didn't have a lot of money when there wasn't a second kid in the house. I was certain Santa would bring me the train. That was the year I learned Santa wasn't real."

That wasn't a memory I wanted to share. But it was tame enough. I suspected a lot of kids had a story like that. But the ache in my chest had shifted. It was sharper now. Harder to ignore.

"Did you find out Santa wasn't real because he didn't bring you the train?"

It took me a minute to make sense of why she'd ask that. "No. Some kid at school told everyone." The question nudged more of a wall I'd built up that I never realized was there. Why did I lump all those details together? How much of my life did I blame on Adam?

Holy shit.

The question stole my thoughts.

Marcie nodded.

That was getting infuriating. How was I supposed to react if she didn't?

"When I was twenty-five, my dad and Adam built me a train set." I *really* didn't want to talk about this. Why couldn't I stop myself. "It was waiting in my apartment on Christmas morning. There wasn't nearly enough room for it."

"How did that make you feel?"

Did she really just ask me that? And why did my trying to figure out the answer feel like gouging out my heart? "My reaction was *who the fuck wants a train set at twenty-five.*" I felt guilty at the memory. "Where the hell was I supposed to keep it? But I didn't say any of that." A knot welled in my chest. I'd been polite, but they both knew I wasn't enthusiastic. "They must have spent hours—days—putting it all together. I was so fucking jealous."

No. Why did I say that?

Because I was. Adam got to spend that time with Dad, and I didn't. They had so much in common.

"What happened to the train?" Marcie asked.

"It's in a box in storage." Another bittersweet memory that was a fist around my heart. This hurt so fucking much. It wasn't fair. "After Dad passed, I pushed it back so far—literally, this isn't a metaphorical thing—that I'd never have to see it again."

There was a lot to unpack in those words. She must have something to say about it.

Nope. She just nodded, and let me keep rambling.

I didn't want to talk about the painful memories anymore, so I shifted to work. At least on that subject I could be furious and tired instead of sad.

I was surprised when she said, "Our time is almost up."

Had it really been an hour?

"How are you feeling?" she asked.

"Like I popped a really big zit. I'm sore. Bled dry. But some of the pressure has been relieved."

She laughed. Apparently she had access to her emotions after all. "That's certainly a graphic visual."

"Am I crazy doc?" I tried to keep my tone light.

"We don't use that word here. But no. You're overworked. You put a lot of pressure on yourself. You're probably dealing with depression. But you're not crazy. Are you coming back in a week?"

No. "Yes."

"Then you have a little homework. I know, nobody likes homework, but this shouldn't be too bad. Think about your job. About the pros and cons of staying."

"I've been doing that for months."

"Do it some more. For me."

As I walked out to my car, my mind was a jumble, filled with all the thoughts I'd had for days. Weeks. Months. All assaulting me at once.

But they didn't hurt as much. And if I focused, I could single any one of them out and set the others aside for a few minutes. I was glad I'd made another appointment.

And fuck, I owed some people some apologies.

As I headed toward home, memories of the train flitted to the forefront of my thoughts. Of my dad and Adam, and just the three of us growing up together.

The sunlight caught the snow and the Christmas decorations. Everywhere I looked, people were hustling, but so many of them were smiling. There was a feeling in the air I couldn't define.

I drove past a craft and hobby shop, and inspiration struck. I took a sharp turn into the parking lot. I knew this place because they had the 3D printer Adam wanted. The one he couldn't afford after he'd spent out the rest of his workshop budget.

Home would wait. My next stop was an antique shop downtown called Deacon's Derelicts & D'art. The ridiculous name made me smile. I'd bet money Adam was there, since his best friend owned the place and Deacon was his fallback go-to.

When I walked into the shop, I wasn't surprised

to see Adam behind the front counter, talking to Deacon.

"Do you have five minutes?" I asked Adam.

He rolled his eyes. "I really don't."

Irritation surged inside and I tempered it. I was tired of being angry. It took so much energy. "I'm sorry." I meant it. "For what I said. For everything."

"Uh-huh."

This sucked. I'd been an ass though, and it was good practice for what would happen with Danny. The more my head cleared, the more I could see how bad I'd gotten over the last few weeks. "Two minutes? And you don't have to like me or forgive me or even talk to me during that time."

"I'll be right back," Adam said to Deacon, then he followed me out to my car.

I opened the back of the SUV. "Merry Christmas." I showed him the printer. "I know you'll do amazing things with it."

"Holy shit." His stunned expression was worth this. "Why?"

"Because I know you'll do amazing things with it." I was repeating myself. Great. "You really are brilliant at what you do. Don't let anyone tell you otherwise."

"What do you want?" Adam eyed me suspiciously.

"Seriously?" I scoffed. "When have I ever praised you for a favor?"

"Never. You don't hand out the praise. Not without a backhanded compliment attached to it."

Maybe Reese was right. Maybe I was more of a Scrooge than Grinch. "There is one thing."

"I knew it."

"*If* you're taking clients, and you're willing to accept extra for a rush job, I want to be the first job you use that for."

Adam studied me, jaw set.

"I swear to you—cross my heart—I'm being genuine. Charge me your rush rate."

He sighed, but a smile peeked through. "Fine. What is it you want?"

I helped Adam move the printer inside, and explained my commission request. When I left, I felt better than I had in a long time. I still had more things to take care of, and this was exhausting, but there was one thing that was more important than anything else. Getting Danny back.

I had a plan and a surprise. To help prove I meant it and this wasn't just words. I needed a little bit of help though. Just a teensy amount.

I called Reese.

"You're lucky I picked up," she greeted me.

Fair point. "Did you tell Danny it was me on the phone?"

"He's not here, but there's no fucking way I'm using your name around him until he's ready."

That hurt. I deserved it. "Will the two of you be at your place Friday night?"

"Christmas Eve? Yes."

Favor time. "When I show up on your doorstep, give me a chance to make things right before you slam the door in my face?" Yes, I called her specifically to ask that.

"What was it you said? Fuck you." There was no anger or power in her retort.

"I'm sorry. About that. About a lot of things." I was going to be apologizing for a while. "Please?"

She sighed. "For Danny. Not for you. Don't make me regret it."

"I won't."

The next few days were eternally long. Almost like waiting for Christmas as a kid, but I was asking Santa for more than I ever had. Fortunately, I had a lot to do to keep my mind busy, and even with Adam's help, we were cutting things close.

Friday night when I knocked on Reese's door, my pulse was hammering in my ears and I was more nervous than I'd been in a long time.

Danny answered. He took one look at me, and shut the door in my face.

32 /
danny

L*et him in.*
   Tell him you don't care about the fight.
Give him a kiss that would break world records.

The words hammered in my ears in time with my pulse.

"You have to talk to him eventually." Reese's voice wove through it all.

She'd known who was out there. Asked me to get the door. I should probably be bothered by that, but I couldn't think past the shock. Past the fear that with Brandon here, I'd do something I regretted.

"I can tell him to go, if you want." Reese stepped past me.

I shook my head and stopped her. "I'll talk to him."

I opened the door to find Brandon still here. I crossed my arms as much to keep him out as the cold.

"Hey." His sheepish smile almost undid me.

This was a bad idea, but now that I was here, looking at him, I couldn't move, not even enough to reply.

Brandon nodded. "Fair. So first of all, very first of all, I'm sorry. Like really, really sorry. I know I've been a little difficult recently. Some might say *unreasonable*..." He looked me in the eye.

If he was waiting for me to correct him, I wouldn't. Not that my vocal cords worked.

"And I'm sorry," he said. "You don't have to forgive me yet. I'm willing to earn back your trust. I'm seeing someone. She's nice. Professionally—*fuck* that sounded bad—I'm seeing a shrink. Not dating someone. The only people I'm interested in are here."

I almost cracked a smile at how flustered he was, and at the implication he was talking about Reese, too, but I wasn't giving him the satisfaction.

"I'm trying. I really am," Brandon said. "And I love you and I miss you and I don't want to lose you and even if you decide to ease back into things with me, at least come back to the house tonight and spend Christmas with us."

"Us?" I looked between him and Reese.

She shrugged.

"Adam and me. He won't be there until morning, because I was embracing hope that you'd come back with me tonight, both of you, but you can join us then instead if you want."

Reese pressed her lips to my ear. "It's up to you," her whisper was so quiet I barely heard it. "Whatever you decide, I'll be with you."

That wasn't helpful. I wanted her to make up my mind for me, so I couldn't blame myself if it went bad.

But she believed in my ability to make this decision, and Brandon looked so sincere. Sounded it. And with the pink kissing his cheeks and sadness etched around his eyes, I didn't want to turn him down.

"I need to know this is more than lip service," I said.

"It is. I don't know how to prove that by promising it, which kind of defeats the point, but I mean it. I have a second therapy appointment next week. You can call her if you want. Not tonight. Maybe not until after the holiday. Don't make me wait that long."

I was tired of hurting, but I was also lost without Brandon, even after just a few days. I didn't see myself getting over him. Ever. "I miss you." The words tasted desperate and right at the same time. "And we'll come back to the house with you."

One corner of Brandon's mouth tugged up in a sheepish smile I rarely saw on him, and I swore the chill melted away.

Reese and I grabbed our coats and bundled into the back of Brandon's SUV. I needed to keep her close, both to anchor me and to remind me. None of us said anything, and the radio was off. With only the crunch of ice under the tires to fill the void, my mind was free to examine the last few minutes.

Brandon's tone was different. His posture. But it was more than that. The accusation was gone.

Spend Christmas with us. Adam and me.

We'd never celebrated Christmas with Adam. Not even the year after their father died, when I thought Brandon and Adam could both use the renewed connection to each other.

And the blame was gone from Brandon's words.

I had no illusions the road ahead would be completely clear, but this all felt like a good start. And I really did miss him. I squeezed Reese's hand —my proof that sometimes giving someone a second chance could be the best thing in the world.

When we got to the house, it was dark out front. Expected. We stepped through the door, and a pale white glow filtered out from the living room. Brandon moved aside and gestured for us to go ahead.

I walked with Reese, but stopped dead in my tracks when everything came into view.

Reese gasped.

Brandon had sectioned off a portion of the living room and put up a train set. Where did he get a fucking train set? It was wrapped around two little houses. One that looked like ours, and one that was more like a stylized gingerbread house.

"I figure it's no fun if you fill out the village the first year," Brandon said quietly. "But I'm hoping we have a lot of years ahead of us to add more."

My words were caught in my throat again, but not because of uncertainty. I looked at Reese. With nothing but Christmas lights reflecting off her awe, she was stunning. The girl I'd always known. The woman she'd become.

I turned to Brandon, who was watching us with a hopeful expression. "Come back home?" he asked.

I nodded, not trusting myself to say anything.

Brandon grinned, gripped the back of my neck, and pressed his mouth to mine.

Falling into the kiss, the familiarity, all of it, *was* home. I kissed back with all I had, memorizing this moment. Searing it into my mind.

"You should realize Reese is part of the deal," I managed when we finally broke apart.

Brandon was smiling. "I wouldn't have dared assume otherwise. Are you staying tonight?"

"And indefinitely." I was here for as long as he kept trying. For as long as all three of us kept growing together.

Brandon pressed a hand lightly to my throat, pushed me to the wall, and smashed his mouth to mine. "The bed feels empty with only me in it," he murmured between hungry kisses.

It was incredible to have our bodies molded together, but I wanted more than making out in the living room. "We should do something about that."

"Couldn't have phrased it any better." Brandon shifted both of us, and used his full body to guide me backwards.

Reese followed, brushing her hand against mine with every step. We reached the bedroom, and she stepped between us, stealing my kisses and my breath before Brandon pulled her to him to kiss her so hard I felt it.

We peeled each other out of our clothes, and the sensation of skin on skin—Brandon's, Reese's—patched cracks in my mind. Reese moved just out of reach and held up a candy cane.

"Should I ask where you were keeping that?" I looked at her with curiosity.

Her nose wrinkled and crinkles formed at the corners of her eyes when she smiled mischievously. "Probably not."

Brandon laughed—the kind of light, carefree sound he hadn't made enough of lately—"She stole it from the tree."

"Busted." Reese snapped the end off the candy, and peeled off the plastic. She popped the sweet into her mouth, then stepped closer again, and kissed me.

The peppermint was hot and cold at the same time, and the playful way her tongue danced with mine redefined Christmas memories. She slid her mouth down my jaw, and kissed along my chest with wet, sticky, peppermint kisses that were hot while her lips were on my skin and icy when she moved away and the air slid in.

She teased one of my nipples with her tongue, and the sensation was intensified.

Brandon kissed me again, licking and nipping my lips then claiming my mouth until the scuff of his unshaven chin burned my skin in the most delicious way. His cock brushed my leg as he pressed in, and I grabbed his shaft.

Reese kissed down my body while I clung to Brandon. When she used her mouth to draw the candy cane along the head of my cock, the minty coolness was almost too much, but it felt so good.

She swallowed my length, and a shock of need tinged with promise filled me. She slid her tongue along my shaft with hungry enthusiasm while Brandon kissed me. While I stroked him.

This was incredible, but I need more. From both of them. I needed to be a part of them. I tugged Reese to her feet, and searched her face. Adoration and brilliance stared back.

"Let me fuck you," I said.

She caught her bottom lip between her teeth. "I've always loved the way you have with words."

She sat on the bed and scooted herself to the middle, gaze never leaving mine.

I reached for a condom, and she stopped me. "I want to feel you," she said. "We're all clean. I'm on birth control. I want you, no barriers, inside me."

I leaned over onto the mattress, hands on either side of her, and brushed my lips over hers. "Yes, ma'am."

She wrapped her arms around my neck and her legs around my waist, kissing me again. We lost our balance and tumbled to the bed in a tangle of limbs and giggles.

"The two of you are so goofy sometimes. *Fuck* I missed this." Brandon knelt next to us, and trailed his mouth along my shoulder.

Reese freed herself enough to press her forehead to his. "I'm glad you figured it out."

"Me too." He kissed her quickly, then pointed her toward me again. "I believe there was mention of fucking?"

"There definitely was." Reese grinned.

I lay her back on the bed, and slid inside her. She felt so incredible wrapped around my cock. Looked so stunning, watching me as I slowly glided in and out.

"Play with yourself," I said. "I love watching the way you touch yourself."

She dipped her fingers between her legs, brushing my shaft as she teased her clit.

I leaned in and pressed my mouth to the shell of her ear. I wanted to take this slowly, but I also wanted everything tonight. We had the rest of our lives ahead of us, all three of us, and I didn't doubt that for a moment, but I needed more *now*.

I straightened and drove myself deeper into her. The expressions that played across her face, the way she licked her lips and her silent gasp of pleasure, were divine.

Brandon pressed into my back, his cock digging into me. This picture wasn't complete without him. He teased slick fingers along my crack, the cold lube warming quickly on my already hot skin.

I paused inside Reese, and Brandon spread my cheeks to penetrate me. And then the three of us were rocking together. Connected in the most intimate way, both physically and through the invisible cord that tied our hearts together.

Reese teased herself faster, her fingers bumping my skin with each stroke, while I fucked her.

Brandon's pace matched mine, striking that right spot inside me, and milking me.

The restraints were gone. I fell into the pleasure of feeling both of them.

Reese's body tensed under me, and I pounded harder. She opened her mouth in a silent scream that became a loud, incredible cry when she came, clenching around me. Squeezing my cock until stars danced behind my eyelids.

Pleasure tightened in my body and caressed my soul. Need surged forward. I hammered harder until I spilled inside her, and even then I kept going, not wanting this moment to end.

Brandon pressed hand to my chest and pulled me into him, letting me stay inside Reese. He fucked hard. Fast. Desperately. And when he came, the sounds he made were the most beautiful final notes in the symphony.

The frantic aura in the room ebbed, but the other feelings, the love and adoration, lingered, as the three of us collapsed next to each other, spent and exhausted. I swore the two of them glowed as brightly as any string of lights.

This was already the best Christmas ever, and I knew each one after this would only be better.

33 /
reese

I was already used to waking up next to Danny again, but it turned out the experience was even better when Brandon was on his other side.

When I stirred, Brandon propped himself up on one elbow to see me. Instead of looking exhausted and strung out, he was smiling. "Merry Christmas. And Happy Birthday."

Danny rolled onto his back, eyes still closed. "Did Santa come?"

"You'd have to ask Mrs. Clause. But you might later if you're naughty." Brandon kissed Danny.

Danny opened one eye. "*Might?*"

This was right. This was what our worlds should be. I sat up, tugging them with me. "I want to go see the tree again. And the houses. And the train. And listen to Christmas music and watch *It's A Wonderful Life*." I thought I'd outgrown the excitement of this morning years ago, but I felt like a girl again. Anxious to greet the day.

"How many times have you already seen it this year?" Brandon asked.

"Not enough."

Brandon smiled. "Don't you want to open presents?"

Presents had never been a big affair in my world. "I left them at my apartment." I was too caught up in the moment last night, too invested in what came next to think about if I should grab them. A fountain pen and notebook for Danny, for poetry-slash song lyrics, and a stack of score sheets for Brandon, for composing.

"We'll grab them later, when I take you both to get your cars." Brand grabbed our hands and tugged us from bed. "Come on."

"I'm in." Danny tossed me a pair of boxers and a T-shirt, which I was more than happy to slip on while they dressed too.

The three of us moved into the living room, and I had to stop at the doorway again and drink in the magic beauty of it all. We worked our way through far more presents under the tree than I was used to. Brandon and Danny insisted it was because it was my birthday too, so that meant double presents.

There were baubles and bigger items—the Gibson for Danny that he'd been drooling over for months, and a new mixing board for Brandon, plus a stunning pair of purple leather Docs for me, from Brandon.

Danny handed me another box to open, and I tore off the paper, to find plain brown cardboard inside. Curious.

I opened it to a lot of bubble wrap and packing peanuts.

"I didn't want anything to happen to it," Danny said.

Brandon chuckled. "Sitting under the tree?"

Danny shrugged. "You never know."

This was so, so perfect. The presents were nice, but the company... Amazing. Especially seeing the two of them together and smiling.

As I peeled off the layers of bubbles, I realized what it was. When I saw the whole thing, I couldn't speak. It was a miniature Hard Rock Cafe, the perfect size to fit in our growing Christmas village, and the little sign said *Featuring Reese Ellis and Plaid Peanut Butter*, in the most delicate tiny script ever.

"I love it." I gave Danny a long hug and kiss. I turned to Brandon. "And I love that there's already a place for it."

"Figure out where it goes," Danny said. "I had Adam make it at the same time as the angel, months ago. I had no idea it would have such a perfect home." He huffed a laugh.

"That explains why he didn't have to think hard

about the base design for the two he made me," Brandon said. "And he never said a word."

"This is all amazing." The warmth inside me probably glowed through my skin. This all felt so good. I set Hard Rock at the end of the street. I was pretty sure zoning laws would require at least a little distance between the houses and the club, even if half the residents were probably made of gingerbread.

Danny kissed me on the forehead. "One more. Be right back." He strode from the room, grabbed a small package from his coat pocket, and returned. "I didn't want you to find it, so I had it tucked away. Which meant it made the trip with us." He handed it to me.

I frowned. This box fit neatly in the palm of my hand. If he'd stuffed it with packing peanuts, that meant *maybe* three of them. I opened it, and nearly dropped it when I saw what was nestled inside. "Oh." The Christmas lights reflected off the gold charm attached to a leather cord. "Is this…"

"Yours. The same one." Danny pulled it from the box and slipped it over my neck.

The pendant hung down far enough for me to hold it in my palm and examine it. Tears clogged my throat—more of those stupid happy ones—and I struggled for something to say.

It was half of a *Friends Forever* charm. We'd gotten them when we were teenagers, and I'd worn mine for years. So did he. It was why it was on the leather cord—I was terrified something like a gold chain would break. When I broke up with Danny, years ago, I'd given him my half back. "I can't believe you still have it."

"I have mine too. It's upstairs."

I threw my arms around him, and squeezed tight, as much to cling to him as to try to hold myself together.

"I love you, Reese," he murmured against my ear.

"I love you too."

Yup. Best Christmas ever.

We were half-assed cleaning up the boxes and paper when someone knocked.

"Perfect timing." Brandon didn't look at all surprised.

"You mean there's more?" I said. "Oh my head."

Danny laughed. "Goof. He said Adam was coming over."

Oh, right. Perfect. Apparently my grin could get broader.

Adam and Brandon made us breakfast—French toast, eggs, bacon, the works. It was part of the tradition at their house growing up. The conversation was stilted between them, but there were no snide comments from Brandon.

A few near misses, but it was obvious he was

trying.

We talked about Adam's plans for his new printer. Where he was setting up, and what he wanted to do next.

Danny caught Brandon up on office gossip, which was a week's worth of silly stories.

Brandon's expression shifted, not to sad, but more contemplative. "Speaking of work, I've been thinking…"

"About what?" Danny's tone was kind and even and free of assumption.

"I'm going to talk to Judith about my stepping back," Brandon said. "Have her find someone else to do sound effects and manage the team, and I'll still do their bigger pieces, but not full time."

Danny smiled. "That sounds like a good idea."

"It means I'll be making less."

"And I'll give you the same reassurance you gave me when I *retired* from cybersecurity," Danny said. "We'll be fine. Hell, we could live strictly off Rinslet dividends at this point."

The mood returned to happy and light as we finished breakfast and cleaned up.

"I'm going to head out," Adam announced. "I'd hate to intrude on Brandon's Magical Manic Boinking time."

I hadn't heard the phrase before, but the lightness in his voice when he said it made it that much more ridiculous and fun.

Adam grabbed his coat and looked at me. "When you need help moving your stuff in, call me."

"I don't know..." I pretended to slide into *thoughtful*. "Adam made me so many pretties, maybe I should be with him."

Between Danny's and Brandon's raised eyebrows and Adam's look of terror, it was nearly impossible for me to keep a straight face.

Adam shook his head so hard I was worried might fall off. "Nope. Don't get me wrong, you're hot, but there's no way I'm coming between you and them."

I wanted to wink and blow him a kiss, but I couldn't hold in the laughter.

"Don't tease him." Brandon's reprimand lacked force.

Adam rolled his eyes. "*Definitely* not getting in the middle of this. Ciao." He waved over his shoulder and walked out the door.

"Speaking of going..." Danny's tone shifted to serious. "I don't want you to, Reese. Go back to your place, that is. Not long term."

I didn't either. Not without them. "Is it weird that I'm already used to waking up next to you?"

"And I have to admit I hate not doing so. Waking up next to both of you." Brandon closed the distance between us, and tilted my chin up. "Thank you for not giving up on me, and for being there for Danny when I was a dick. I'm so glad you're you, and that you came back into his life—our lives—and I love you. It kind of scares me, but in a good way, because I love you as much as I do Danny, just in a different way."

Now I understood exactly how the Grinch's heart grew three sizes. The swelling in my chest was an amazing feeling, and I had to be lighting up the room from my glow. I rose on my toes and brushed my lips over his. "I love you too. So much, even though we're the most soap opera worthy threesome ever. Pretty sure this was a plot in *Days of Our Lives.*"

Brandon smirked. "Or a Heart song."

"Holy goddess." Inspiration struck. "I know how the song ends." I grabbed both their hands and tugged them toward the music room.

Brandon pulled us to a stop. "I should warn you before you go in there." He winced.

He hadn't. My drums? I tugged away and ran into the room, pulling up short when I saw they weren't there, and neither were most of the guitars.

"I promise they're all right." Brandon's sheepish voice came from behind. "I couldn't look at them, but I couldn't hurt them either. They're in the shed."

I'd known the situation was bad, but his confession drove home *how bad.* Thankfully we were moving past that.

"I'll bring them in now." Brandon turned away.

I grabbed his arm. "Later. We just need the piano and guitar." I sat on the bench and pulled him next to me. "You both remember this." I played the opening notes from the Cinderella song.

Brandon picked up the top half of the music and Danny joined in on the acoustic guitar. As we played through, I told the story again, to refresh it in my mind and help set the mood. When we reached the end, I kept going. There was one more stanza to add.

The handsome prince realizes he can't live without his confidant or his Cinderella, so he joins them.

Danny had only been dabbling with lyrics last time we talked about this, but as we reached the chorus, he had words.

As he sang, I knew this would be a chorus that would shift as the song went on. I sang along with him when he repeated it, and Brandon accompanied us.

I leaned into Brandon for the next repeat, and moved to stand next to Danny for the last.

This was so perfect. Maybe fame came next— probably but possibly not—but it didn't matter. This moment, what Danny, Brandon, and I had, was a better future than I ever could've written for myself. My best friend and childhood love, his prince, and the three of us living happily ever after.

epilogue

One year later
Brandon

It was strange to have an early Christmas planned with Adam. In past years, we would've just skipped it, but after last Christmas, after all the healing we'd done since, I didn't want to miss out on another holiday with him.

But he had plans over the holiday and so did I. The compromise was Christmas morning, but three weeks early. Danny and Reese insisted this was time for just the two of us.

It was easy to fall into the old tradition of making breakfast together, and swapping banter while we ate, and then moved to presents.

I was excited to see if Adam liked what I got him, but I'd save that for last. He handed me a small box wrapped in shiny metallic paper. I didn't have the patience to open the package slowly, and ripped off the paper instead.

When I opened the box inside, I swore I stopped breathing for a moment.

It was a flatcar—an open bed train car with no sides or top—with a grand piano in one corner. A tiny bench sat next to it, with a little person painted like me. The floor of the car was hand painted with a few bars of the first piece of video game music I'd ever composed.

"There's no way a piano would travel like that." I knew without question that would've been Dad's argument against making the train car.

"And yet, this was his idea. He just never got to…"

I didn't need Adam to finish the thought. The two of us had gone through a lot of therapy in the last year, some together and most separately, but some topics were still tough to navigate. I couldn't talk past the lump in my throat, so I gave him a tight hug.

When we broke apart, I cleared my throat. "I'm feeling a little reciprocal gift inadequate, now."

"Well, hand it over and let me judge for myself." His voice was thick.

I grabbed my phone from my pocket and scrolled through the images.

"So…" Adam sucked on his teeth. "If you got me a picture, that *might* be a little… Yeah."

I looked at him, eyebrows raised. "Thanks, smart ass." I meant it with nothing but love. "It was too big to wrap, but it's waiting at your shop." I showed him the photo of the sign I'd had made, for said new shop.

He grinned. "It's perfect. I assume it is anyway."

"It's even better in person. I promise."

Adam gave me another hug. "Thank you."

I squeezed back, then stepped away. "Go. Check out the sign. Do your thing. Call me when you land."

"I will."

If I looked back, I could see those moments where I started to slip and fall apart, but I didn't do as much looking back these days. I preferred to see the potential in front of me. And I couldn't have gotten here without Danny's support. Without Reese's.

Speaking of... I needed to meet them at the Salt Palace, watch their equipment check for tomorrow's RinCon opening night. I'd dreaded RinCon a year ago, and now it was one more thing that proved we had so much of our lives ahead of us.

I couldn't wait to experience all of it, with the people I loved by my side.

Danny

Reese's and my childhood dreams never included *Headlining one of the biggest gaming conventions in the country*, but I loved that it was happening, and so did she.

We stood on stage, a curtain between us and the opening night celebration audience. Reese was on drums, with a mic next to her for singing, I was on lead guitar, and we had two new members—Maddox on bass, and Alys on drums, backing up Reese when she stepped out to take center stage.

Brandon didn't perform with us, but he was as much responsible for the music as Reese, and he mixed all our masters.

The soft glow of light that filtered around the edges of the curtains vanished, and the dull roar on the other side dropped to a hush. The curtain rose, with faint lights playing around us, but keeping the band in shadows.

Reese started off with a simple beat, just three drums, and the instant I slid into the opening chord for *Glass Slipper*, the crowd went nuts.

We didn't do many covers these days, and never as our first song, ever since the band took off. We weren't *playing stadiums* big, but we opened locally for some bigger names, and people knew our name.

This song technically made us. It had been almost a year since I wrote the lyrics to Reese's Cinderella story. Once Brandon and Dustin got us on video, got the sound right, and got the video online, things built from there.

From *Glass Slipper,* Reese joined me at the mic, and we moved into a few other songs by us, and then the *big deal* for this show. Brandon joined us on piano for the covers of the AcesPlayed songs, that I'd written lyrics to, and we had the main theme from Rinslet's newest game in the mix too.

The excitement in the room was tangible, and Reese glowed. If they shut off the lights, her energy could probably brighten the stage on its own.

Reese leaned in closer, sharing my mic, pressing her cheek to mine. The fans were awesome, and I knew she loved them, but the one thing that mattered most to me was being on stage with her. With Brandon a part of this.

When the performance ended, Reese was practically buzzing with energy and it was giving me a contact high. The curtain closed us off from the fans, but I wasn't surprised to find a large number of people waiting for us backstage.

A lot of them wanted autographs, and several of them were in Plaid Peanut Butter shirts. Adrienne and Phillip had made digital versions of the outfits we performed in, as bonus content for the launch of the game, and there were a few people cosplaying as us. How surreal was that?

One girl in a *Reese* jacket that she'd made herself

approached shyly and asked if the entire band would sign her coat. Reese beamed, signed first, then passed around the sharpie.

"Excuse me." A smooth, quiet voice interrupted when I was done signing.

I turned to see a young man who was *maybe* in his early twenties, wearing a leather bomber jacket that looked a lot like mine, with a guitar that almost looked real hanging on a strap around his neck.

How surreal was this? Someone was cosplaying as *me*. "Hi." I gave him a warm smile. "What can I do for you?"

He shoved the foam instrument at me. "Can you sign this? Just you."

"Sure." I turned the guitar over in my hands. "This is amazing work. Did you do this?"

He blushed and ducked his head. "Yeah."

"Wow." I found a good spot on the back, where the coloring was lighter, and signed my name plus a short message. "Keep up the good work."

"Can I ask you something?" He took the guitar and put it back on again.

"Sure."

"The song is real, isn't it? You and your prince found your Cinderella?"

Our relationship wasn't a secret. I glanced at Reese, who was busy signing everything anyone put in her face, and Brandon watching from the sidelines, then back at not-me. "It is."

"My dad says what you're doing is disgusting and never works out."

It probably wouldn't for his dad. "Do you agree?"

"No."

"Good." I grinned. "If you want to love one person, or two, or fifty, that's up to you. Never listen to anyone who tries to squash that in you."

"Thank you." He was already vanishing into the crowds.

Someone pressed into my back and wrapped their arms around my waist. "Mini-you. Too adorable," Brandon said.

"With any luck, his journey won't hurt as much." Not that I'd surrender what I had—who I had—for anything. I leaned my weight against him and pulled his arms tighter, while I watched Reese working her way through autographs. She looked at us with a smile, then turned back to her fans.

This was all perfect, the way the three of us were meant to be.

Reese

As the group of our fans thinned and dissipated, the buzz of another amazing show still thrummed in my veins. Danny and Brandon joined me, and

Danny nodded toward the escalator. "We have company."

Adrienne waved, then rested her hand on her belly. She was pregnant enough to pop, and I'd never seen her happier. I also had no idea how she'd managed working at all today, but she insisted she was fine as long as she was careful.

That hadn't stopped Dustin and Phillip from sticking her in a chair every time they saw her. Apparently it was the best compromise the three could make.

We joined her. "Hey, happy momma," I said.

Her smile grew. If being on stage made me glow, she outshone me by a thousand watts. "You guys were amazing tonight."

"Of course we were."

Brandon scoffed, but he was smiling too.

"And I'm glad I got to you before you left," Adrienne said. "We wanted to talk to you, but Dustin got pulled away, then Phillip had to go help, and they made me stay here…" She blew out a puff of air. "God, I'm *so bored*."

"Poor baby has to be good for her baby." I was sympathetic, rather than mocking.

Adrienne laughed. "Which was why we—or just me now—wanted to talk to you. The three of us were talking…" She twisted her fingers together and sighed. "We want the three of you to be the baby's godparents."

The offer pinged in my heart, and felt better than all the applause in the world. "Are you serious?"

She nodded.

"I can't speak for them, but I'd be honored," I said.

Danny squeezed one of my hands, and Brandon the other. "Same." They spoke together.

"Yay." Adrienne hugged me tight. "Not that I thought you'd say *no*, but there's always some doubt. And you'll all be perfect, and you've really become just the most amazing friend." She snapped her jaw shut, and stepped back sheepishly. "And *yay*."

We chatted with her some more, made sure she was delivered safely back to Phillip, then headed out. The warmth in my chest spread through all of me, as I thought about her request. About the men by my side.

When I lost Mom, when I lost Danny, I had decided I was safer alone.

I was so glad I'd learned since then. So grateful to have this new family.

———

Thank you for reading Reese, Danny, and Brandon's story.

For more AcesPlayed fun, grab MATCH-MAKING IN PROGRESS. Sonya knows Jeremy and Quentin are perfect for each other, she just has to prove the same to them. As she pushes them together, she realizes she's falling for them. But when they realize she's been keeping a secret, she may lose them both.